THE

TATTOO

WIDOW

BECKY PARISOTTO

◆ FriesenPress

One Printers Way
Altona, MB R0G 0B0
Canada

www.friesenpress.com

Copyright © 2021 by Becky Parisotto
First Edition — 2021

ISBN
978-1-03-911231-5 (Hardcover)
978-1-03-911230-8 (Paperback)
978-1-03-911232-2 (eBook)

1. FICTION, LITERARY

Distributed to the trade by The Ingram Book Company

Dedicated to D.

Ride Free.

PROLOGUE

I killed my grandmother when I was sixteen. My family wouldn't agree, but I know it was me. I put my shoes on the bed with disregard, without a care, and the next morning she was dead. She told me a hundred times to never put shoes on the bed. A warning for what was to come.

She was the first dead person I had ever seen. Laying on her back with her eyes closed, I remember searching her withdrawn face for something familiar. I studied her loose cheeks, pulled down by gravity; they looked like the dull surface of sculpted clay dried in the sun. I examined her large pores, filled and smoothed with makeup, applied coldly by the mortician; makeup she never would have worn. My eyes danced across her chin, scrutinizing the surface for the small, wiry hairs I desperately wanted to see there still. The ones she asked me to pluck as her eyesight worsened. Gone. My chest felt like an old wristwatch that had been wound up; the pressure and ticking in my ears were the only real moments I could focus on in the room as the rest of my family crowded near me, touching my arms and shoulders and openly weeping, dramatizing the event. My eyes were dry, my mind, dry, and my being as empty as hers. I felt drained of blood as if my body had been cut open, the cavities emptied and replaced by wax molds of each organ to preserve the spaces for later, for when I would come back to life.

CHAPTER 1

To try and understand me would be a mistake. I don't have any answers for you because I can hardly understand myself. Indexing my thoughts, I watched my feet hit the ground, taking the familiar strides to my destination. The steps were taken by memory, but the feeling of discomfort always rose to the surface. Catching my reflection in the windowpane, I sucked my cheeks in and lightly bit down with my molars, thinking it would contour my face.

I could barely see the low red glow of the sign as I traveled down the street. It looked like a television, projecting scenes from the next room, a halo of activities you were excluded from yet were tempted to walk over to and try to observe. I focused on the young group of teenagers gathered in the neighboring alcove on the sidewalk; they wore layers of ill-fitting clothing, heads covered, each with a cigarette to their lips. I passed them or others like them every day walking down this same street and always felt out of place. I concentrated on the tempo of my heels striking the uneven sidewalk, each step buckled and bloated with tree roots creeping through. I clutched my scarf closely to my chest with my free hand, though it wasn't chilly out, and kept my face turned down to avoid conversation. As I reached the edge of the building on the north side of the street, my eyes searched the exterior brick for the small, familiar piece of graffiti that signified the arrival at my daily destination. It said, "get fukd," in poorly executed dingy white text, no bigger than a classroom eraser. My eyes hunted for it every time I arrived and rounded the corner to the door.

A vibration flirted in my ears, like raising your lips close to the edge of a grass reed and blowing in quick bursts. The familiar anxious nerves sat around my collarbone like a delicate necklace made of filigreed gold. I pulled open the barred glass door under the glowing neon sign that cast red light across my forearm as I reached for the handle.

As I entered the shop, the loud music momentarily spilled onto the street until the door quickly rushed shut behind me. My eyes scanned the familiar scene as I took inventory of the day's activities. I could hear the low and fast buzzing of machines running through the air in unison, pausing out of sync and controlling the vibrations of the room. My nostrils were filled with the potent scent of CaviCide, the powerful medical cleanser that sterilized the previous actions of each customer, washing away their story before the next client arrived. A deep knot tightened in the pit of my stomach while my gaze surveyed the room, the flesh of my cheeks still pinched between my teeth.

Each station was occupied with a person folded in a unique and balanced position, holding as still as possible while their tattooer crouched over them in concentration and focus. The artists all wore black t-shirts, their backs hunched; it reminded me of a pod of whales moving tightly together in the waves, communicating with each other through the vibration of the machines in their hands.

I looked across the room to the wall hung heavily with artwork. My eyes darted quickly to a new small addition to the collection of paintings, drawings, musical instruments, small figurines, and sculptures on the wall. The assemblage showed a history of years of stories and gifts brought by clients and friends, extended out to the artists like a dowry for their daughters.

I walked over to the new piece nestled between two large frames, and crouched slightly to get as close as possible to the creature. The corners of my mouth pulled down with concentration. I discovered a bat—a common bat, hanging upside down by a pin in the wall in petrified splendor. It was no bigger than my thumb, its skin tight and dry and striated with fine bones and muscles beneath the surface. Moving closer, I noticed the four pointed, seemingly, sharp teeth displayed in its open jaw. I examined the fine hair on its snout. The bat appeared ugly and frozen in death, and was now part of our collection without its consent. Unframed, and free for me to touch as I reached my finger toward its wizened, filmy skin. Letting the tip of my finger barely rest upon the minuscule top tooth, I felt a stab of disappointment, discovering the tooth's point to be dull. I was dispirited by the lack of reaction from the dead predator. I pressed slightly harder, realizing how easily I could crush this tiny, preserved creature. The temptation to do so proved to be overwhelming. Straightening up, I spun my body toward the room, cautious of the finger that had touched the bat's mouth at my side, not letting it rest on my leg.

My eyes found my reflection staring back at me in the gilded mirror that hung next to the bat. My shoulder-length brown hair pulled tightly into a low ponytail, the line of my faint lips punctuated with small creases on either side. I leaned in closer, examining the bits of concealer caught in the fine wrinkles under my eyes. I patted the skin gently with my pinky finger to try and smooth it out. *You look plain*, I thought. *You do not look special.* My skin was pale, clear, and smooth but showed that I was no longer in my twenties, and the harsh bright lights of the tattoo shop highlighted the details that I worked to mask. Running my hand over my hair, I pressed my palm tightly to my head to flatten the small whips escaping around the crown of my head. I pulled my sweater away from my body self-consciously, not wanting it to cling to my middle. Catching my own gaze, a sharply edged triangle of light clung to each iris as I stared at myself; the geometric highlights looked like tiny knives. Squeezing my lids tightly shut, I waited to see if a stabbing sensation would arrive. Behind my eyelids, a cascade of shapes appeared against a black background, forming rows of crescent moons in a fuzzy night sky.

"How do I become invisible?" I whispered, not moving my lips, the words sitting in my mouth, overflowing at the corners. The light bent around my shoulders and the shape of my legs; it closed up around my back and down my spine. The shadows migrated back toward my feet, dissolving with each inch. The reflection of my form in the mirror dulled, moving to the bottom of the frame until it disintegrated. Gone. I was fully camouflaged, hidden in the spotty outer space behind my eyelids, a tiny knife waiting behind each to defend me. With my shadows turned to peppered flecks of darkened shapes, I fit perfectly onto a single wavelength of light, cloaked and hidden on this instant of unibandwidth, holding perfectly still. If only I had the power to choose who can see me. Forcing them to see me. To make them only see me—and to be hidden from the rest, at will. I slowed my breathing and could feel my body sway slightly side to side at the shoulders, fighting to keep this moment of invisibility with me. I released the tension from my eyelids, dreading the instant of reopening and losing the power of veiled protection. The light stung my retinas, and my pupils narrowed quickly. I was back. Looking past my reflection and over to the room behind me, I drew in a long breath.

I moved across the brightly lit parlor, working my way through the maze of bodies toward the back corner. As I approached his station, he looked up at me without raising his head, but rather only his gaze for a flicker of a second, machine continually running in hand without pause. The expression on his face barely changed as he digested my arrival, the thin line of his mouth not visible through a heavy beard as I got closer to his side while he worked.

A smile moved across my lips, "hey," as I stopped near his shoulder, cautious not to touch him.

"He-llo," Dylan replied in the sing-song tone he always used with me in front of customers.

It was not his normal voice, but I expected it each day as I entered the shop. He intently pressed a line into a young woman's calf muscle with black ink, swiftly following the path of his perfectly positioned stencil, born from a drawing he had poured over for hours the night before at the cluttered desk in the corner of our living room. I examined the progress, watching the small muscles flex in her ankle from the pain as Dylan pulled the needle through her skin to complete the shape. As he lifted the machine away from her leg, I noticed her foot relax. He turned to me and looked up.

I placed my hand on his shoulder for only a second and moved it across the slope of his back, the finger I'd touched the bat with slightly hovering off his body. The silent space left by the quieting of the machine as audible as the buzz. My visit had no purpose; they never did. I would simply go for the sake of going, to remain on the inside, fighting hard to do so. If I didn't go, I wouldn't see Dylan for days on end as he'd be at the shop, head down, tattooing without a care for the rest of the moving world—myself included.

He looked like he'd aged overnight, like a three-day-old balloon forgotten from a party that still has its color, but now showed wrinkles and creases and the surface no longer taut. He dressed, as always, in a uniform of dark t-shirt and jeans, boots that were never cared for, and a beanie to cover his balding head. His arms were swept in a long, light blanket of blonde hairs, swirling over years of tattoos decorating his skin, the hair slightly blurring the images as if you were squinting to recognize a friend from a distance, unsure if it was them. The tattoos that showed out of his sleeves were layered in blues with touches of skin peeking through. The once-solid black outlines had begun to fade, creeping away like dust beneath the surface. Examining his arm, which I had seen for fifteen years without any regard for its imagery or symbolism, made me suddenly self-conscious of the bareness of my own skin. I reached for my wrist and rubbed the absent clean space quickly. Moving my arms behind my back, I clasped two fingers to hold them in place and out of view.

"What are you doing here?" Dylan lightly questioned, without malice.

"Just wanted to see you," I replied, my typical response to this same question.

An empty inquiry, the type you ask a stranger when you have no intention of listening to the answer. Letting the conversation skip off my surface, I focused on the artwork underway.

The young woman lay on her side, facing away from Dylan's gaze with her leg extended to him as an offering. There were smears of black ink across her skin, stippled with blood gathering like an hourglass, marking the time it had taken for us to interact. The lines were forming a chrysanthemum flower, fine in its detail and execution.

My eyes traveled to the girl's hair, seeing it fall in small golden yellow strands across her face, much like the individual petals of the flower being imprinted on her body. I searched the rest of her frame, wondering if she had any concept of the artwork she received from Dylan.

The flower comes from Eastern tattooing roots, symbolizing perfection and deity. I imagined this young girl dressed as royalty, draped in the rich colors and fabrics of the throne. Standing at her feet, I thought it an appropriate place for a peasant wife of the royal adorner to be stationed during this intimate ritual. My mind transformed her hair into thick long braids which dressed the table upon which her body spread, offering herself to my husband for touch, but nothing more.

"Why did you choose a chrysanthemum?" I innocently asked the girl, waiting to form judgment on her lack of knowledge of the history of her selected imagery.

I had developed a jaded disdain for all the reasons people professed behind their selected permanent badges; these empty excuses for their images fueled my intense research of tattooing antiquity and culture to make up for the lack of artwork on my own body. My skin, bare and obvious when inside the walls of the shop we had built together. Shifting the weight between my hips, I awaited her reply. The pressure gathered on the balls of my feet as my toes slid forward into my high-heeled shoes, which felt noticeably inappropriate for the setting.

"Oh, well, my grandmother grew them, and I just like them because of that," she responded, quietly and without moving to see who posed the question.

When she said grandmother, I swallowed the word out of the air and tried to force it down into my lungs, but it felt sharp and stabbed my breath as it tried to enter my body.

My grandmother was a gardener too, and religiously planted yellow chrysanthemums gently between the rows of tomatoes growing in her sloped yard. "It's to keep the beetles away," she would declare to me while waving her hand dismissively at my question when I asked why she did this each year.

She always wore the same brown dress while in her garden, thick and shaped like a box that covered her rounded center and large shapeless breasts. The dress hung to the middle of her shins unceremoniously. Sticking out of the bottom of the weighty dark tarping were her soft and swollen ankles, broad with creases and folds while being tightly bound in thick stockings, which she wore daily to cover the small web of purple and blue veins patterning the surface of her skin like a map of rivers on the landscape. Her sandals were beige, crossed leather with a small Velcro strap to the side; my eyes were always drawn to her feet to examine the tumid toes cased in hosiery protruding beyond the edge of her shoe, one toe folding over the next encroaching on the limited space provided.

"Put-a your finger in the dirt here for me," she instructed, her accent making the syllables dance, as I took short and light steps across the uneven yard to arrive at her demand.

I crouched down low, careful to not disrupt her tomato plants close behind my heels, and I pressed two fingers firmly into the earth while balanced on the front of my feet.

"Like you-a mean it! Make room for the roots," she instructed forcefully as I swirled my fingers deeper into the soil to make space for the young flower to sit, feeling the grit collect under my fingernails. "You need to-a fall in love with the roots, Bambina, not with the blossom; the roots hold the light, and the petals are just the image," she mumbled to me as she tenderly stepped through the vegetable bed to hand me the sturdy, small shoot.

My mind snapped back to the present moment. I stared into the mesmerizing eye of the blossom, admiring its intense symmetry and self-healing powers.

"Ye-ll-ow," I mouthed slowly to myself as I placed the bloom into the fresh crevasse and swept the earth to its edges for support.

My gaze scanned the static flower on the young girl's leg; I stared at her body blankly as if she were a corpse.

I began wondering if Dylan remembered he once brought home these same flowers a few years into our relationship. I tried to shut off the seed of memory and not allow it to enter my brain, to catch the light and open its mouth for water. I could not hold it back as it slowly spread across the front of my mind. It was the only time he ever came home with flowers in all these years. That afternoon, when I saw the shadow of his shoulder pressing into the screen door of our old house with the periwinkle siding and grey trim where we had lived simply, I stopped what I was doing and observed him without his knowing.

I remembered the feeling of confusion and a twinge of lightness seeing the small, neat bouquet of yellow mums in his hand. He pushed into the mesh of the window, pressing hard enough to cause the feeble wooden frame to bounce in place, long enough to catch his toe under its edge and flip the door toward himself with his foot. A reflexive maneuver he'd honed over years of rehearsal. I held still, not offering to help, practicing my reaction to his gift in my thoughts.

"For me?" I resounded, trying to sound light and mask my thrill as he stepped up into the kitchen, the well-worn floor plank groaning beneath the weight of his foot.

"What's that?" Dylan responded, a welcoming and innocent smile on his young face.

"Flowers" I declared, softly gesturing toward the posy tightly clasped in his large hand.

His gaze darted involuntarily between his hand and my eyes as he connected the question to his thoughts.

"Oh, yeah, no, just at the market on my way home just now, and they had these! Can you believe it? Chrysanthemums! I'm tattooing a Japanese sleeve next week, and I'm going to tie it together using chrysanthemums; I saw these flowers and thought I'd grab them to do my drawing study from. Cool, hey?" The excitement in his voice over his find hung in the air between us.

"Yes, really gorgeous, good plan," I hummed, trying to echo his enthusiasm without showing in my face the disappointment that washed over me.

Turning back to the sink, I reflexively grabbed a rag to busy my hands. I should have known better than to believe he had thought to bring me flowers. I wasn't the type of woman that needed validation, I told myself. Walking to him, I reached for the arrangement and began searching the kitchen for a jar large enough to support the blossoms, placing them delicately to the side of his drawing table like a trophy marking second place in a spelling bee.

I fixed my eyes back down on her leg. Dylan refocused with fresh ink sitting in the end of the needle, guiding it in and out of the pale dermis. One hand piloting the coiled machine across her thin extremity, the other hand applying pressure to stretch the skin tightly to allow the needle to enter with accuracy.

Picturing her tattoo on her now-taut calf, I could see it as she ages and grows into an elderly woman, the same age as my grandmother, with her body transformed by time. I see this tattoo on Nonna's calf, hidden safely behind her stockings from the rest of the world. The flesh of this young girl's leg now solid and shiny, eventually dulling with age and beginning to look like the finely patterned surface of a drought-riddled dune, with detailed cracks and lines. Each perfect petal wilting with her years and dusted with a glaze of lingering skin awaiting its renewal. I imagine licking my finger and pulling it from my mouth, leaving a metallic taste on my tongue, reaching out to her aging leg and running the moisture over the center of her tattoo. A glistening track is left behind, watering the flower and bringing a small streak temporarily back to life to this moment, lying on the table, feeling the pain of the needle.

"Well, it's looking beautiful," I whispered to her, offering no feeling.

I put no effort into my comments to most of Dylan's clients. I didn't care if I saw them again after all these years of various men and women lying before him. Seekers never surprised me anymore. He adorned the young and the old, the educated, the poor, students, executives, and many gorgeous young females willing to permanently mark their bodies as a reminder of this moment in their lives. I didn't learn their names; I didn't ask for their stories—I didn't care. I looked at them as money; I wondered how long they could endure the pain of the process and how many hours of work they would pay for. That's all that mattered to me now after so many years.

Not to Dylan, though. Dylan was never the type to learn names and make emotional connections with others, but he didn't think of the money either; he connected to each drawing and how it became a tattoo. The machine worked just as an extension of his body at this point. The soft vibration controlled by his foot, surging the adjusted power through his leg, up the cord, and into his fingertips.

Dylan morphed into a man controlled by his vices, and tattooing had evolved into his main drug, his body longing for the rush of anesthetization. The high he felt came from the control, the attention, the accolades, and the admiration. He breathed in the strokes of strangers traveling across the world to sit at his fingers, to throw their bodies at him, and pay for his time to pretend like they were friends, to pretend like they were forging a bond through this experience. Dylan never bonded with anyone. He was a very closed man, smart and observing, but rarely participated with others. He laid his hands on people's bodies all day, touched them, stroked them, inflicted pain upon them, and he felt nothing for them in the slightest, but he stole their energy. He thrived off of it silently. Their blind veneration filled up his emotional well, though he worked tirelessly not to let it show. He was a man composed of finely balanced layers of ego, constantly battling to not allow it to drown out his soul. He compensated when the scales swung too far, but rarely noticed when they did. It was his loudest flaw and the root of who he'd become.

I stared at his profile until my eyes blurred, the brown and red hairs of his beard turning into a shapeless shadow hanging onto his chest. Fighting to stop myself from blinking, the burning in my eyes caused them to narrow. I fixed my gaze on him until the hurt became too much and I couldn't recognize him any longer. I closed my lids tightly and squeezed until the rush of relief subsided and I felt normal again.

"Okay, bye Dyl. I will see you tonight or tomorrow, depending," I ended, as I headed back for the door without him looking up to acknowledge my departure.

Pushing open the door secured with the wrought iron bars, I let the music seal off the world as it closed behind me.

CHAPTER 2

"Why did you show up today, Annalise?" Dylan questioned. We were sitting at the dinner table, which was tucked off to the side of the narrow kitchen. Two windows met at the corner; the frames had been painted multiple times over the house's life, leaving a thick and textured layer in the cracks that looked like frosting.

"I—I, I just wanted to say hello, I guess." Stammering, I searched for the words, swinging my hand in an actioned gesture.

"What the fuck is wrong with you, Annalise?!" Dylan screamed, spit forming at the corners of his mouth.

I felt the words hit my face, clinging to my throat, running their nails down my chest.

"Wh-what?" I stuttered, backing my chair away from the table.

"What the fuck?" Dylan shouted, his eyes widening. I had spilled my wine, flailing my hands, animating my defense.

"It was an accident," I whimpered, my eyes lowered to the wooden surface, unconsciously examining the line down the center of the table where you'd pull it apart to place a leaf when all of your family would be gathered around. There were small flecks of crumbs stuck in it, maybe black pepper. I reached up and ran my fingernail down the crack, collecting the history of our meal and flicking it onto the floor.

"Accident? Well, you ruined my pants, and you ruined my dinner!" he bleated, not noticing my state of mind.

Only seeing red. Red wine. Red behind his eyes. Blood red. I rose slowly from the table, reaching for a rag in the sink to clean the mess. I heard Dylan shove his chair back with anger, clanging on the wooden floor as he stormed from the room. I took the opportunity of his absence to quickly clean the evidence of my mistake. My hand shook as I lifted his plate to absorb the residue of the wine from under his dish. His fork rattled off the edge and landed sharply on the tabletop. I heard him walking down the hall, back toward the kitchen, as my chest tightened.

"There," he said.

He sat back down on his chair, wearing a fresh outfit. He reached out and grabbed my wrist as I finished cleaning up the spill. I tensed, afraid he would lash out.

"It's okay," he said, as a small twinge of relief filled my lungs.

Dylan's reactions were always unpredictable; this I knew. But I also knew his anger was always as temporary as cheap nail polish. He stopped my hand from cleaning until I looked up at him.

"Hey," he cooed, sensing the worry in my body.

Lifting himself off his seat, he moved toward my mouth, opening his lips to kiss me, leaving the taste of wine and garlic on my mouth. I stiffened, trying to keep him calm. I felt his strong hand tighten around my wrist, but only for a quick pulse.

"I'm going to the shop," he whispered, his beard moving on my cheek as he spoke.

He slid his feet into his unlaced boots while pulling on his jacket. I saw him reaching for his motorcycle helmet, signaling he likely wasn't going to the shop, but rather out for a ride. I never knew where he went; I only knew that he'd leave for hours or sometimes days at a time without any contact. He'd return without mention of his whereabouts, and never acknowledge the length of time he'd been gone for. I always felt relief when he left for a few moments, which soon transformed into worry. I worried not for his safety, but rather for the anticipation of his unannounced return.

I'd spend days with heightened hearing, expecting every noise to result in the screen door bouncing open and his heavily treaded boots traipsing on the hardwood plank. My ears would reach out into the street, searching for the low echoing pop of his pipes as he downshifted to take the corner to the back alley to our house. I'd wait. I'd listen. I'd lay awake at night, anxious for his return and dreading the sound of passing motorbikes. I wanted him to come home so I didn't have to think about him coming home.

Standing at the sink, scraping the remnants of dinner into the basin, I heard the motorbike fire up outside. The familiar rumble entered my feet as he cracked the pipes to warm the engine. As he accelerated down the street, I heard the long, low-oboe cry signal his departure until he turned the block, out of range. Finishing the dishes, I stared out the window above the sink.

Outside, there was a small flower bed I had planted with a delicate fig tree a few months earlier but never tended to it. In the low remaining summer light, I could see the silhouettes of dried stems and lifeless leaves that had once been shiny and proud and healthy. I reached for a mixing bowl that sat on the counter, dirty from preparing dinner. Dunking it into the soapy water in the basin, it was mixed with bits of food, and brown in color from the remaining wine. I balanced the bowl, watching the water slosh from side to side, spilling over and running down my arms, the soap itching. Pressing open the door with my hip, I walked around the corner of the house to the flower bed below the window. I quickly dumped the water over the lifeless, dead fig stems, causing specks of dirt to splash and stick to my bare feet and shins. Setting the bowl on the edge of the rotting wooden frame, I returned to the house, locking the door behind me.

Morning came, and I examined my reflection in the oval mirror hanging in our entryway over the small table holding my keys and a pile of dusty loose change. I straightened my yellow scarf and smoothed the front of my sweater, critiquing my choices this morning. I leaned in close to the mirror, again examining the creases at the corners of my mouth that had taken up permanent residence there, no matter my expression. Touching the thin skin under my eyes, I recognized the purple-colored hue that had patterned my Nonna's face. Dark and thick hair pulled back loosely at the base of my neck.

As I leaned toward my image, my eyes flickered to the bottom corner of the mirror. Through it, I could see that sitting on the step outside of the door, was Dylan. A small start caused me to jump in place, though I could only see the back of his head. I hadn't heard the motorbike return last night as I drifted in and out of sleep. I quickly reached for my keys and bag and opened the door.

"Hey, morning," I offered, reaching down to touch his shoulder as I sat on the cold cement next to him.

"Hi," he replied, turning his face to mine.

"You're home," I said, relief in my voice.

I wanted him to come back, and I wanted him to leave forever. I had this thought every time he took off. Wanting a cowardly excuse to start fresh, I imagined a disaster on his motorcycle where he never returned, everyone felt sorry for me, and I didn't have to explain why we were no longer together. I felt the shame of this familiar thought creeping into my mind.

"Yeah, I'm home. I need to get showered and get to the shop," he said, rubbing his hand over his forearm, massaging the ever-aching tendon near his elbow that had deteriorated from years of tattooing and was awakened by holding the throttle at speed on the bike.

My eyes glanced over, and I saw the bandage sticking out of the cuff of his plaid button-down flannel shirt.

"What's that?" I asked, knowing the answer.

"Oh, I ended up over at Craig's shop," he affirmed, pulling up his sleeve to reveal a blue bandage wrapping around his wrist, secured in place with tape.

He picked at the corner of the tape, pulling back the bandage with tender care. Stipples of blood began to appear as the covering gave way and fresh air rushed to the wound. He extended his arm over toward me, revealing a perfectly scripted and tightly coiled letter "A" nestled into the tiniest of corners on his wrist, in a spot crowded with years of imagery, converging at this same point on his body. The "A" faced him, and as he extended it toward me, it pointed at my chest like an arrow. My eyes focused on the bloodied wrapping he'd discarded on the ground, a perfect blood-and-ink-stained letter sitting in exact reflection, staring up at me, soaked into the bandage.

"Ouch," slipped out of my mouth and stuck in the tight space between us.

Pushing myself off the cool cement step, I felt the rough surface poking into my palms and looked down at the uneven brick as I walked toward the gate to the street, heading to work.

CHAPTER 3

I had worked at The Easel for six years. Six and a half, to be exact. I had moved from my twenties to my thirties silently within the walls of the bookstore, having seen the same faces for nearly 2000 days of my life, enshrined by books. I had made unacknowledged friendships with patrons, assigning them names in my mind based on their appearance and their consistent selections.

The Easel was a bookstore carrying new and old art books, stacked tightly to the ceiling in dusty, used, mismatched shelving. The books were categorized by period, genre, artist, year. They were organized to force exploration and curiosity.

The aisles demanded that you browse down each one and required you to enter without a purpose. The precarious arrangement of heavily bound hardcover offerings showed off their spines and the occasional cover to the hundreds of sets of eyes that scanned them daily, begging to be touched and turned and taken home.

I had love affairs with various books within these walls—some that I casually dated and entertained, and some with which I entered long-term relationships. Closing my eyes, I recalled a book's placement on a shelf, the weight of it, and the page number containing my favorite images. My loyalty would sway between tomes, between periods in history and artists over the years, as I explored and learned the residence on the shelves.

As customers would walk toward the teeming and hidden register near the back of the enclosed store, I'd feel my breath tighten in anticipation, hoping they were not purchasing a book I'd come to depend upon. Of all the books within the walls of The Easel, I had a best-loved volume that I had tucked away to ensure it would never leave me. The publication felt oversized with a light cream dust cover, slightly dirtied on the edges with micro-tears from picking it up and not expecting the weight. It was marked on the cover with fluid calligraphic sweeps depicting Japanese characters that I could not translate. They were tangles of fine glossy lines that danced on the cover, but looked deeply embedded and burned into the book's surface.

It contained drawings from Japanese tattoo master Horiyoshi III. The pages were filled with delicate and complex pen and ink lines, creating traditional dynamic masterpieces depicting dragons, demons, and mythical creatures from Japanese lore. The book was void of color, just black ink, and the artist's hand. I'd turn to the most well-worn page in the book, of which I'd respectfully dog-eared the corner only slightly, for quick access. Sliding my finger between the pages, I turned the weight to the side to reveal the drawing in anticipation. A full-page Fudo

Myo-o illustration using all the space the page had to offer. I studied the pages of this book day over day, tracing my finger over the major compositional lines of each drawing, imagining the ink flowing from the tip of my finger effortlessly to create these contorted sketches.

I knew nothing of Japanese culture, people, traditions, families, art, food, or countryside, but I knew everything about this book. My people were Italian, and their people were Italian. We didn't venture a single degree away from our roots, but I felt magnetized by this book and I knew exactly why. It was a portal to Dylan's mind, a snapshot of what drove him to put pen to paper each day, ink to skin. Tattooers found their place in either the sailor culture of port cities and prostitutes or in the fine art and ceremony of Japanese descent. For Dylan, always the latter. He studied the drawings, the history, the books, the people. He listened to the traditions coming up in old-school shops about the Tebori technique, pushing the ink into the skin by hand with a needled stick without the assistance of a coil machine, bringing to life classic peonies, kois, dragons, tenyo, and blossoms to transform bodies into shapely canvases, deepened with shadows and displaying tapestries for eyes to devour.

Dylan obsessively learned the Buddhist imagery; he always needed to be an expert in each avenue of interest in his life until it consumed him. His propensity to become addicted to even the healthiest acts, such as learning, could become destructive. He could recite the deities on command, though he'd never speak of these learnings, but rather mentally correct others' inaccuracies and then tell me at length the detailed corrections in private later, second hand.

The Fudo Myo-o had always been his favorite. It was the image that covered his own back, shoulder to shoulder, from the nape of his neck to the lines and patterns tucking neatly under the cheeks of his bottom to cap off the natural line of the body. The highly detailed rendering of Fudo Myo-o bore into his dermis with perfect craftsmanship, flowing with the natural muscles and lines of the body, lifelike as his body moved. The imagery seemed aggressive, terrifying, and strong—and accurate. Dylan. No one ever saw this masterpiece other than me; Dylan had always been a private man about his tattoos, never wanting to discuss them or share in the experience with others. The only people he ever discussed tattoos with were other tattooers, and me.

Even though my skin sat bare, I'd earned his respect through studying the history and profession with such intensity that he knew I'd understand. I learned each painful detail not for him, but for myself - I needed to decode his mind, and this seemed like a logical starting point.

Fudo Myo-o has a terrifying appearance at first glance. His face is contorted with a menacing grimace and two fangs protruding from the corners of his fouled mouth. One fang pointing up, with the other twisted down. A hardened third eye, and donning dark blue, nearly blackened skin, his form perches him proud upon a rock, always surrounded by flames, confusing the uneducated viewer. His hair falls to the side in a thick braid like a strong lariat present. But Fudo Myo-o played a gentle and kind protector. The flames, in fact, stood to represent the burning of anger and the fire of passion to purify the mind. He sits strong on a rock to show his determination, and clutches a rope in one hand to capture and bind demons, and a Kurikara sword in his other hand, he uses to subdue the devil and cut through ignorance. The turned fangs point up toward truth and down to show unlimited compassion for those suffering. Fudo Myo-o is a misconceived symbol, often mistaken for a demon. The literal translation means "the immovable wisdom king." A guardian of Buddhism, and the central figure of the Five Wisdom Kings of this faith.

Misunderstood.

The center of his own universe. Surrounded by flames and made of stone.

Misunderstood.

Remembering the first time I found this book, it sat tucked away in a small section piled high with covers depicting Japanese gardens, lanterns, and origami. I almost didn't open it that day as I remember the cover seeming underwhelming and uninviting. Dirty and tired and lacking all appeal.

As I began flipping through the pages, a slow and dangerous enlightenment crept over my skin. I had found Dylan's secrets fully illustrated and awaiting my translation. I snuck back several times throughout the day to scan the book; my heartbeat in my ears with each turning page. It took me a full week to read each translated page within the binding, learning about Horiyoshi III as a master tattoo artist in Japan, and trying to make clear the tangled myths and riddles of Japanese Buddhism.

All I had known of religion was as a child, sitting in Catholic church next to my Nonna each Sunday morning. I dreaded this task. I'd sit on the end of the sturdy oak pew and hang my arm over the side into the aisle. Routered into the flank of the pew was a symmetrical pattern, closing in a four-leafed clover. I'd run my finger around and trace this formation in a slow, steady motion for the hour's service until the tip of my finger became so numb, I could no longer feel it. Near the end of each service, the congregation would rise and we'd shake hands with the other patrons near us. We'd whisper in low voices, "peace be with you," shaking the outstretched palms vigorously, but only so far as you could reach without leaving your station. My finger would be completely numb by this stage in the weekly ritual, so that as I extended my hand to lightly shake those around me, I felt nothing in this protruding digit. Slowly, the finger would regain feeling, being spiked by pins and needles and bringing on a small wave of discomfort and anticipated pain. I'd dig the fingernail from my thumb into the tingling finger over and over until it had returned to normal, examining the small crescent indentations left behind by my nail.

I neatly arranged my mysterious illustrated find away in a corner of the store which was not frequented often. I slid the trophy between two copies of the same book, *Art History in the 20th Century.* A dry journal chronicling the recent revolutions in the visual world. Turning the book with the pages facing out, I hid the spine, tucking it away to ensure no one would be tempted by the calligraphy flowing down the binding. The next morning, I returned to work an hour early and started again at the first page of the book, seated cross-legged on the floor, casting a shadow over the pages with my body.

The time passed quickly as I began to build a story in my mind surrounding these pictures and the artist's hand from which they'd come. Horiyoshi III, the apprentice of Horiyoshi II, I learned, son of Shodai Horiyoshi. Horiyoshi III, or Yoshihito Nakano by birth, became the second apprentice in 1971 at age twenty-five in Yokohama, Japan. I studied the small black and white image of him printed modestly inside the dust cover of the book. Tiny printed dots made up the form of his serene face like a printed picture in a newspaper obituary. The text under his small portrait read: *Horiyoshi III is the second tattooist to be granted that honorific name from the Horiyoshi dynasty, passed from master to apprentice. The tattooist affixation hori means to engrave or to carve. When asked how he'd describe his work, Horiyoshi III stated: 'The creatures I draw only come alive on somebody's skin. This is why I never show my designs as so-called art. I draw simply for fun and to have samples to show my clients so they can pick a new design. The creatures depicted take the person's breath away once they are on his or her skin—and then the two start breathing together, in unison. Human history alters the look of the animals and plants I paint, and when the person wearing them dies, so too do they.'*

As I read this, cold flushed over my entire body. *"When the person wearing them dies, so too do they,"* I read again, allowing my eyes to linger on this sentence, repeating it in my head over and over until the words stopped making sense and they were merely sounds.

I heard a book slide to the floor, the familiar slap of pages landing with its full surface flat on the worn tiles echoing through the shallow hallway. I quickly glanced up, realizing the store had opened and it had been a patron who had nudged the book off the table near me. Searching for her eyes as my vision adjusted to looking up to the light and away from the page, I closed the book over my hand to preserve my place. An elderly woman nodded slowly to me to apologize for the abrupt interruption. I noticed her to be Asian in descent, her distinct hair shiny and straight, hanging like a curtain from a snug-fitting knit cap. Her gaze seemed gentle as she looked down into my lap, turning her head slowly to the side to process the calligraphy on the cover of my book.

"Crows and Herons," she said, smiling with her entire face as she translated the sweeping text on the front of my prized possession.

"P-pardon me?" I stuttered, not realizing her comment to be a transcription of the cover.

She gestured at the flowing ink. "Crows and Herons," she repeated with certainty.

"Oh, is that what this says?" I queried, my voice rising in interest, running my fingers along the glossy shapes.

"Hai," she nodded, confirming our exchange.

She chuckled, running her speckled hand over the projected shape of her belly in a slow single stroke.

"Do you know this story, *ko*?" she cooed.

"N-no," I said, my gaze darting between her and the book.

She took a step closer and reached for my shoulder. She braced herself as she bent and knelt beside me, sitting on her heels with comfort. She licked her top lip out of habit and pressed her mouth together into a line until it disappeared completely. She let out a steady breath and began.

"In Ujjain, in India just outside of town there lived the most impressive fig tree in the entire nation. In this tree lived two birds. One a generous heron and the other, a wicked crow. Though by nature, they were not meant to relate, they enjoyed each other's company and lived in this powerful fig tree together." She paused, reaching out and tapping the top character depicted on the book I clutched tightly to my legs.

"On a very warm summer's day, a weathered traveler stopped to seek the cool shade of the fig tree and rest. He set his bow and arrow down next to him and propped himself under the canopy to close his eyes. After a lengthy sleep, the shadow of the tree had shifted and left the sun to beat down on the exposed face of the guest," she adjusted her weight a bit in her crouched position. "The sun interrupted the tired traveler, and he could not rest peacefully. With his kind heart, the heron noticed the discomfort and spread out his wings to protect the man from the sun. The wicked crow watched from his perch, and it was not in his nature to help others. He especially disliked others to be happy."

Her voice sang gravelly but strong, and my ears reached for the next words to come from her mouth.

"The fiendish crow did not want another to find pleasure under his tree, and he took delight in troubling others. The traveler shifted and opened his mouth to yawn, and the crow relieved himself into the mouth of the guest and flew off!" She motioned her hand off into the distance, her voice high and strong. "The man jumped to his feet, riddled with anger, and searched above him in the fig branches. He spotted the heron, wings spread, and mistook him as the delinquent." The woman lowered her eyes for a moment before shooting back and locking my stare.

She motioned with her arms, pulling an imaginary arrow from her quiver, and loading it into her bow, she squinted and closed one eye, taking aim into the distance.

"He picked up his bow and arrow, and he shot the heron, dead." Her voice was flat, matter-of-fact in purpose.

"My family has a saying, little one," she offered, touching the back of my hand only for a moment. Her fingers felt like dry crêpe paper.

"The company of the crow only kills the heron." With that, she reached for my shoulder and pushed herself back to her feet easily.

She shuffled over to the next row of books, turning sideways to fit past the other patrons in the tight aisle. I listened to her windbreaker swoosh with each swing of her arm.

CHAPTER 4

*D*ylan never invited me to ride on the back of his motorcycle. In ten years, I've never wrapped my arms around his body and held on while the pressure of the wind tried to fight me off him. He spent hundreds of hours alone on that bike. It didn't even have a back seat.

The bike was a Harley Davidson, stripped of all its logos, brand markings, chrome, and glamour. Painted flat black like that of an old barbeque forgotten in the corner of a yard without grass. The front forks had been raked out and extended just beyond comfortable reach with the handlebars traded for ape hangers, forcing the hands over chest height into an unnatural position. The pipes were wrapped in a flat metal mesh, upgraded from stock to Vance and Hines to provide that powerful, intimidating rumble envied by all other men on their bikes and despised by any person that didn't ride. Dylan had removed the signal lights and foot-boards, and had lowered the bike a few inches. As he cornered at speed, his pipes would touch the ground creating a small spray of sparks. The ride felt stiff, uncomfortable, and impractical—exactly what he wanted.

"What time are we meeting for dinner tonight?" I asked Dylan as he looked down at his phone, scrolling through the night's happenings the next morning, frozen in place as the doorway to the kitchen.

No reply.

"Dyl, what time are we meeting for dinner?" I repeated, with a heavy emphasis on his name.

"Huh?" he replied, no answer provided.

"Dinner, what time should I be ready for dinner?" I stated, staring at him focused on his device.

"Six, meet you there at six," he muttered.

Grabbing my shoulder bag off the table, I marched to the door without a goodbye. I'm not sure how I arrived at The Easel that morning; I followed my typical path, but I don't remember the streets, turns, or roots in the sidewalk where they always live. Arriving at the front door on autopilot, I pushed open the heavy wood and glass door covered in smudged fingerprints, tiny indicators of each visitor from the past few days. The door closed behind me with its familiar exhale, accompanied by the moan from the bottom hinge and the satisfying click of the latch catching and settling into place. Relaxed, I was enveloped by my daily ritual.

Standing behind the front desk, I stared at the calendar hanging on the wall, a few degrees off level. June 21st, the first day of summer; the solstice, the longest day of the year. The month's picture illustrated three horses running through a wheat-colored field. The background blurred in motion, the speed of their hooves a streak across the bottom of the image. The corner of the calendar bent as if stored in a drawer that fit too narrowly for its shape, but was forced closed anyway.

Dylan obsessed over summer solstice every year; he hated the short hours of daylight that closed in on his shop, on his house, and on his mind in the late days of fall and through the blackened winter. I, too, grew to look forward to this event each year, when the earth tilted on its axis, its face closest to the sun, to pause and feel the spread of warmth crawl across its surface.

When we first met, we used to count down to this day of the calendar. The first year in our house with the periwinkle siding, Dylan danced into the kitchen unannounced, chanting. I spun on my heel to see him without his shirt, less many years of tattoos, with a pink bath towel tucked around his waist. He had tied my scarf to his head and began performing a ritualistic primitive dance of sorts.

"To the pagan Gods!" he yelled, between drum beats he rhythmed on his thighs, and high-pitched screams and yelps hopping between each foot, stifling back giggles.

Standing there in shock, I covered my eyes with my hands, and laughter escaped my mouth. "Summer solstice!" he screamed, "where the days are long, and the light is warm, and commoners can celebrate without shame!"

I ran to him and threw both arms around his neck, launching myself around his torso. He supported my weight, and we danced around the kitchen, continuing our chant to the sun standing still for a day. Ever since that first summer solstice, we always marked the day by sharing a joint on the back steps and staying out on the porch wrapped together to enjoy every moment of light. As the years passed, our tradition barely clung to the calendar, but that memory stayed bright.

This year, I asked Dylan to celebrate the summer solstice with dinner at his favorite Mexican restaurant.

"I invited Holly and Ben; it will be fun! They have a patio so we can stay out until the sun goes down and drink their watery margaritas!" I dampened my enthusiasm; I remembered Dylan dancing around, sacrificing to the pagan sunshine Gods, hoping he'd be happy with the idea and wanting to see that same memory creep across his mind.

"Yeah, okay, cool," he had said when I asked, no indication of his primal dance appearing in his mind's eye.

Six p.m. arrived, and I sat on the back patio of Jose's Casa with Ben and Holly across from me. The table was covered in a cheap vinyl tablecloth, the cotton batting poking through a hole burned through by a drip of wax from the Virgin of Guadalupe candle placed in the center of the table.

Plastic lights were strung overhead between tables in the shape of small and glowing red peppers. My legs stuck to the back of the white plastic chair beneath the bottom of my skirt. I looked down to see my thighs flattened and the tiny hairs sticking up as the planet began to turn its face away from the sun, fighting to hold on for me, waiting for Dylan to arrive to enjoy the extra minutes of warmth together. I glanced to the doorway, willing him to fill the frame, but the clock ticked on, and the sun began to sink a minute at a time toward the second-longest day of the year.

"Dylan doesn't run on the same clock as the rest of us, hey?" Ben joked, a drink in his hand.

As always, I stopped looking over and began to settle into the evening, forgetting the empty chair, the extra minutes of daylight, and focusing on the friends in front of me and the servers arriving with our food. Feeling a hand on my shoulder, I jumped slightly, stopping mid-sentence to turn. Dylan stood over me, walking around the table to hug and greet our company. Looking at my phone, it read 7:33 p.m.

"You made it," I said, strained through a tightened smile.

"Hi!" Holly said, standing to lightly hug Dylan with half of her body.

Going places alone is something I've become accustomed to; Dylan rolling in hours late unapologetically or not showing up at all because he's gotten carried away on a tattoo happened nearly weekly, and it didn't make me flinch anymore. Dylan sat quickly, reaching over to my plate, and began to share my dinner and my margarita. He grabbed the corner of my plate and pulled it between us. Familiar purple stains were visible along the rim of his fingernail on his index finger, the transferred ink from the stencil paper filling the space around his cuticle bed.

"This food is fucken terrible," he mumbled, tossing the soft tortilla shell back onto my plate, a spec of sauce flicking onto my lap.

I watched the red sauce seep into my skirt, a ring of translucent oil forming around its edge, no bigger than the size of a pea.

The extra minutes of daylight passed without acknowledgment; Dylan kept busy with the waiter, ordering tequila shots for the table. The liquor arrived and everyone toasted and grimaced as the amber liquid burned. I didn't drink mine, and Dylan reached over without comment, tossing it down his open throat. He reached across and grabbed the margarita in front of my plate, removed the straw, and gulped down the murky green drink. I could hear his words and thoughts beginning to slow down. I could see his blinks lengthening, and he caught a spoon with his hand, letting it clatter to the floor without comment. I placed my hand on his thigh under the table and gave it a slight squeeze; my ears became flush with nervousness.

"Dyl," I whispered. No reply. "Dyl!" I said again, my teeth clenched. I leaned my forehead onto his shoulder for a moment.

"What?" he snapped, jerking his shoulder in the air, roughly dismissing my touch. My eyes danced between our friends across the table; they shifted in their seats with discomfort, knowing what was to come.

"Nothing, all good," I retracted, smiling while I clasped my hands together in my lap, looking down at them.

"Hey, guys, everything is okay. Dyl's here now, so let's just enjoy ourselves." Ben stepped in to moderate, lifting his drink nervously. Holly shifted uncomfortably in her seat.

"No, Annalise, what's the problem?" Dylan shouted. "I've been at work for twelve hours; if I want to come here and have a drink, I can! You drag me to this shitty restaurant and parade me around, and then you think you're going to tell me how to act?" He spat the words at me, causing me to lean back in my chair to avoid the shrapnel.

"It's nothing Dyl, really . . ." I stammered, looking around the room, noticing the stares coming my way.

"What, you think I give a fuck about what these losers think?" he motioned his arm in the air, referring to the tables near us with patrons staring our way, heads turned for the show.

He shoved the table, shaking the drinks and knocking the candle onto the plastic tablecloth, its hazy red wax trickling over the edge. His chair made a brief screeching sound as it scooted across the patio tile and clambered over onto its side.

"Fuck this!" He grabbed his helmet and stomped away to the exit.

I didn't look over at him; I knew to wait a moment. Grabbing my purse, my hand shook as adrenaline coursed through my arms and I rummaged for my wallet. I pulled out a $100 bill that I had neatly folded for the occasion; I had been saving it from a birthday card my parents had sent me in the mail in April. Tossing it onto the table, I ran to the exit on my toes to avoid my shoes making any sound as I escaped.

CHAPTER 5

I didn't see Dylan for eight days. When he reappeared at the house, he made no mention of his absence. He walked to me sitting in my reading chair pushed into the corner of our crowded living room and kissed me roughly on the temple; his beard stabbing my face caused me to wince. He didn't say a word to me. I watched him in the reflection of the hallway mirror. He pulled clothes from a pile at the foot of the bed and changed into a fresh black t-shirt. I watched his body as he contorted to get his arm and head through the openings at the same time. He looked old; he looked damaged.

He pulled the bedroom door closed behind him heavily and powered down the hall, striking his heels with each step. I heard him pause and shuffle back to the door frame of the living room.

"Hey," he offered, hanging his head and torso into the room, leaning back cautiously while grasping the edge of the old lath and plaster wall.

"Yeah?" my voice cracked, having not used it in two days.

"I don't want to do this," he cleared his throat to force the words out.

"Do what?" I asked, desperate for him to walk all the way into the room, to square his shoulders to me.

"Any of this," he said, pulling his body from the frame, continuing down the hall.

Hearing the screen door bounce on its hinges behind him. Holding my breath, my ears reached for the sound of his Harley starting up on the street.

Getting up from the chair, I stood quickly and felt the pins and needles in my feet from being curled up. I felt the clenching in my throat as tears welled in my eyes and built up the pressure in my forehead. I pulled the quilt from the chair and looped it around my arm to stop it from dragging onto the floor. I entered the bedroom and looked at his t-shirt discarded on the floor at the end of the bed. Kicking it with the side of my foot to clear the path, I crawled into bed. Pulling the quilt over my head, I left a small sliver of light to allow my breath to escape as the tears ran across my nose and puddled in the crease between my ear and the pillow.

Reaching for the nightstand, I felt around for my phone. I pulled it under the blanket with me and turned it on; the light screen blurred with tears. Finding Dylan's last message to me, all it read was *ok* dated eleven days prior. He never replied when I sent him messages. I texted him *I love you* and leaned the phone on the edge of the bed, pressing send with the side of my thumb. I heard the small whooshing noise as the message went out into the universe and found its way to his pocket. I watched the screen and saw the word *delivered* under my message. After a few minutes, it changed to *read*. Knowing he received it, I knew he wouldn't reply.

My eyes flooded with tears, and I could feel my chest getting so tight. I don't know how long I lay there, salty liquids running into my nose and mouth; eventually tired, I fell asleep. Waking a few hours later, I reached for my phone, pressing the power button to check for messages—no reply.

I let the phone slide from my hand and get tangled into the bedding as I rolled to face Dylan's side of the bed. My body fit neatly tucked onto my side, awaiting his presence. Reaching my arm under his pillow to feel for a cool spot, my hand brushed a bundle of hard objects. I sat up on my elbow and pulled the pillow away, pushing it onto the floor. Looking down, I saw seven cylinders staring up at me. They were rolls of cash, held in place by tiny black elastic bands used to hold the needle firm to the body of the tattoo machine. I reached for one and wasn't able to get my fingers wrapped around it. Turning it to its side, I saw it was wrapped with a $50 bill on the outside. I started to shake, tossing the money onto the bed.

CHAPTER 6

I knew Dylan wasn't coming home. That's all I thought, at that moment. I pictured him on his motorbike riding away from me and our house and our life. I didn't consider the details beyond that of where he would go or the logistics of him coming home and separating our lives. I could just see this anonymous figure dressed in black leather riding away on the road alone like a cliché in a movie, the sound of his pipes fading into the horizon. It wasn't that simple. He did come home, in fact.

I could feel the pregnant silence filling the room as I ran my fingertips over the texture of the wool sectional sofa in a dulling rhythm until they lost all feeling.

"Annalise?" the gentle voice toned, pulling me from my stare.

"Annalise, did you hear my question?" her voice registering, I jerked my gaze to her.

"How do you die?" I asked her, without intonation.

"P-pardon me?" she returned, taken aback by my change in direction.

"Well, you're a doctor, aren't you? How do you die? What do you feel when you die?" I demanded of her, meeting her eyes for the first time that day.

"Umm, well, Annalise, we both know I'm not that type of doctor. I'm a psychologist, Annalise. I do not perform medical procedures and such," she said, nodding her chin forward as she flexed her neck muscles, the skin clinging to the tendons showing themselves to me like tree branches that had grown thick and spiny over the years.

"I don't want to see you anymore," I told Dr. Fletcher, my voice quivering as I let the words slip from the corner of my mouth.

I looked down to the sleeve of the old sweatshirt I wore, a small tear in the cuff. Burrowing my pinky into the hole, I spun it around as I heard the threads strain and break.

"Well, you and I both know that it's a requirement of receiving Dylan's life insurance money," Dr. Fletcher offered, sympathy in her words.

"I don't care," I mouthed. The words formed on my lips, but were not audible, even to myself.

Looking up, I held her eyes, the corners of my mouth shaking and pulling down as I fought off tears.

"I can just see his feet," I stammered as I fought hard to keep the image from building in my memory.

"Feet?" Dr. Fletcher questioned as she wrote quickly on her notepad, looking down into her lap.

"Yeah, his boots. They were really dusty." I offered her this detail, never having disclosed it to anyone before.

I squeezed my eyelids shut as tightly as I could, trying to stop the image in its tracks.

"Where were these boots worn, Annalise?" Dr. Fletcher's voice was soothing and cautious.

Lacing my fingers together, I squeezed until my knuckles became white and the joints burned.

"When I found him. I saw them through the small window in the garage's side door. I thought it strange he'd leave without those boots; he wore them every day . . . but he didn't leave without them." I waited, but as I peeled back this small layer of the truth, I felt relief slip out.

"I saw them quickly, and then I did a double-take as I noticed them twirling, kind of slowly." I ran both of my rough hands over my face quickly, pulling the skin down around my eyes.

"I saw his feet dangling," my voice was breaking. I bit down into my lower lip as hard as I could, pinching the skin with my teeth until I tasted the tinge of blood on my tongue.

"What do you think they did with his boots?" I questioned, looking up at Dr. Fletcher's furrowed brow.

"I like those boots," I said, lifting my finger to my lip to check for blood. It had stopped, and I gently sucked my lower lip into my mouth in a slow rhythm.

"Have you seen someone die?" I prompted her. She didn't respond. Sitting in this office, the air thickened between us. I closed my eyes, pressing my tongue to the roof of my mouth, trying to block the air from my throat. A memory took over.

"Nonna, have you seen a dead body?" I asked her enthusiastically, grabbing onto the end of her apron string to get her attention.

She stood at the counter preparing jars for canning, a frequent ritual performed to line the shelves of her cold room down in the basement with preserves to last for months, or even years.

"Annalise!" she exclaimed, spinning on her heel in my direction.

She clutched quickly for the cross which hung around her neck from a heavy gold box chain, sharing space with an Italian horn for luck, and a charm of St. Francis. She pulled it to her lips, planting a dramatic kiss upon it.

Using this same hand with the charm still in place, she made the sign of the cross quickly and muttered "*perdonarla*" while her eyes searched the ceiling. "Forgive her," she asked of God on my behalf.

"*Sta'zitto!*" she said firmly to me and swatted my hand away from the apron string.

"Nooooo, Nonnie," I whined, "I mean it! Have you ever seen a dead person? Me and Carmina—no —Carmina and I, we went into the cemetery last week! We read all the names on the rocks, and we saw them digging a hole. I bet it was for Mr. Tosonno; he died, you know."

Speaking quickly, standing to her side, I looked at the loose skin under her chin. She tilted her head down to the counter, drying the rims of each canning jar carefully with the edge of her apron.

"They found him in his house, and he wasn't wearing any pants!" I exclaimed, my eyes widening, waiting for her reaction.

"Bella, death is-a no-funny business," she replied in a low tone. "It will-a sit on your shoulders and stop you from-a moving."

"Well, how do you get rid of it?" I queried, scrunching my forehead and nose in confusion. I tried to imagine myself carrying Mr. Tosonno, and I couldn't figure out how that would work.

"It-a don't leave you, Bella," she turned her face to me and let a small smile take hold of one side of her mouth. "It will stay. You just learn to-a let it live with you."

I had no idea what she was talking about.

Carmina and I had squealed at the sight of the earth being disturbed at the Glenmerry Cemetery. She dared me to run over to the grave and touch the pile of soil that had formed near the new burial site.

"Do it!" she urged, shoving my shoulder lightly from behind, causing my body to flood with adrenaline.

"No!" I hollered, knowing I would do it anyway.

"You're a chicken!" she shouted, taunting me to run over there.

"I am not!" I replied and dug my heel into the grass beneath me.

I pushed off and pumped my arms while running across the browning grass. I could feel my pink cotton shorts sliding up my legs and bunching at the crotch where my thighs rubbed together.

My heart pounded in my ears as I approached the dirt pile, and I reached my hand out toward it like a football player fighting off incoming defensemen. I touched the earth and turned at the same time. Dirt slid down into the ankle of my sock and shoe, and rubbed on my soft skin as I ran back to Carmina full of excitement. We squealed and clasped hands, jumping in place.

"I think the body was already in the hole!" I exaggerated, knowing well and good that the hole proved empty. "I saw it! I saw Mr. Tosonno, and his body looked blue!" We screeched louder at the thought of his rigid dead corpse laying out in the dirt for all to see. "It wasn't even scary," I bragged as we lowered our locked fingers and let our grasp come loose. "Death doesn't freak me out at all," I gloated, glancing back over my shoulder at the dirt pile in the middle of the cemetery.

I looked down at my finger and noticed the halo of dirt stuck under my fingernail. I shook my hand vigorously at my side, trying to fling the dirt from its tight hiding place under my nail and in my cuticle.

It stuck to me with ease.

CHAPTER 7

Thirty-six. Thirty-six days. That's the number of days it had been since I had last been to the house, since I had last been to The Easel, and since I had last seen Dylan's feet hanging in view through the garage door's small and dirty window. For thirty-six days, every person in my life had come to touch me, to watch me, to feed me, clothe me, wash me, and speak the most delicate sentences to me.

Thirty-six days of tattooers, their wives, and clients from a decade's worth of work all reaching for me. Thirty-six days of sleeping in my childhood bed, of my mother hovering near me, constantly on the edge of melting down. Thirty-six days of people telling me, "well, you just can't go back to that house," and insisting that I must "sell that tattoo shop," being looked after by the apprentice and friends and artists from every corner of our past coming to lend a hand. Thirty-six days of "I'm so sorry for your loss," and others avoiding eye contact at the market, and of pained expressions of sympathy.

My hair looked matted with filth as my mother took my head into her lap and gently brushed out each small tangle with such tenderness and a tiny black comb missing two teeth near the end.

She ran her hand over my oily mane away from my ear as I heard her catch a sharp sob in her throat. I couldn't feel anything, just complete emptiness; utterly hollow. I filled the spot with self-loathing and other people's pity. I filled the spot with tears and screams and pills to make me sleep. I filled the spot with an ache so deep that it pulsed into my toes and throbbed so far down into my stomach that I'd grasp at my skin and try to pull it from my body. Thirty-six days of the same day being played again and again on repeat, the needle at the end of the record waiting to be set back to the first groove and starting over again. Thirty-six days of Dylan's boots being the first image to build in my mind as I awoke from bits and pieces of sleep through the night.

Day thirty-seven arrived, without invitation, and settled into the bedroom where I'd closed in so many nights before. My parents built this house in 1978; they bought the property after their modest wedding and built a practical split-level home with three bedrooms and two bathrooms. The yard was proudly full and loved, and the walls inside were covered with neatly framed family photos. Rolling to my side, I looked up at the plastic stars I'd stuck to the ceiling in my youth that would catch light through the day and let off a dull glow as night arrived. My mother had left my room untouched. A full-length mirror in the corner of the tight room stood freely on the floor, framed proudly in an amber-colored oak. My grandfather had made this for me for Christmas when I was very young, along with one for each of his granddaughters. I'd stuck a small decorative sticker in the top corner, which had peeled away from the sun over the years and only left behind the dingy white residue, turned grey with age. I rolled to my back and closed my eyes; I noticed I wasn't crying, and a nervous wash covered my body. I took in a deep breath through my nostrils and let it seep down into my chest.

"Nonna," I murmured.

Wishing she was here to speak with and tell me that life would be okay again.

"Nonna." I sighed, feeling the pain gather and the familiar flood creeping in.

CHAPTER 8

"*N*onna, who is your best friend?" I questioned as I sat on the edge of the counter in her dark and cramped kitchen on Astoria Drive.

I had loved to watch her work in the kitchen, to track her movements from side to side of the L-shaped countertops, scattered with ingredients and tools. She had her back to me; I focused on the strings tied into a lopsided bow from her apron. Her thick torso rolled over the edges of the ties, absorbed into the folds.

"What do you mean my best friend, Bella? Your Nonno, he-a my-a best-a friend." She raised her hand in the air, holding the dull knife she used to section cod up for the night's dinner of baccala.

"Noooo, Nonna. Not Nonno. Not your husband, your best friend. Like a girl." I challenged her, drawing out my sentence into a whine.

"I-a have my sister, and my bambinos, and your Nonno. I no need anyone," she stated, dismissively.

"I have a best friend," I answered, even though she didn't ask the question. "Carmina, Carmina Rosemary Risolli. She's seven just like me, but she's taller, and she has arm hair," I state proudly.

I looked down quickly to my feet, remembering I wore Carmina's worn leather shoes; the left toe was so scuffed that the color had been removed and the tip of the sole ground flush with the hide. I swung my feet unconsciously, darting my eyes back and forth between each foot.

My heel struck the cupboard front as I gained momentum, and Nonna jumped with drama and hollered, "*Sta'zitto! Diavola!*" I clutched my knee caps to slow the swinging limbs immediately. "*Preggo, preggo,*" she muttered as her broad shoulders moved without notice over the fish on the countertop.

"Nonna, what does heartbreak feel like?" I asked, for no reason.

She was old, and I figured she had the answers to questions you couldn't look up in books at the library. She stopped. I heard the paring knife clank on the countertop, vibrating back and forth until it came to rest. Nonna turned her whole body toward me and stared for a long while. I looked at the deep purple circles under her eyes, not from fatigue, but from the thin skin surrounding her irises, allowing for the capillaries to show through, a sign of her ancestors. I reached up to my eye and touched the skin underneath my lashes, recognizing the familiar coloring; I had the same.

"Why, Bella?" she whispered, her entire voice a concerned question.

"I don't know," I shrugged.

"It . . . it-a feel like self-destruction, Bambina."

I didn't know what that meant. Her hand reached behind her, searching for the edge of the countertop to rest her palm upon, as if for stability.

"Heartbreak make-a-you life feel like you been in a lie, and everyone know about the lie, but you no-know. *Tutti!*" she exclaimed with more drama than I expected.

Feeling a tiny pump of adrenaline hit my veins, I didn't know what she would say or do.

"Nonna?" I sang, raising my voice to get her attention.

"Bella, heartbreak is not a word I can tell you about; it is a place you live. It-a make a home for you, and you want to move out of that-a home, but you have-a to stay. You and-a try and pack, but you stay." She busied her hands again.

I had no idea what made me ask this question, the innocent thought just popped into my mind, and I felt I needed an answer.

"Bella, go and get my tweezers, I have-a hair on-a my cheek and a me-a no see it so good in the mirror! I need-a you to take it out before I go to the church!"

I hopped off the counter, feeling confused. Is heartbreak a place you live? How could this be? Looking down at the linoleum floor as I doddled to the bathroom, careful not to step on the lines in the pattern.

"*Andiamo!*" I heard Nonna shouting from the other room, as I stepped into the bathroom searching for her tweezers.

A small gold tube in the cabinet above the sink housed Nonna's lipstick; it was the same tube that had been in there for my entire life. Opening the lid with a satisfying pop, I lifted the dusty rose stick to my nose. I took in a deep breath to smell the medicinal odor. Twisting the bottom of the tube until the color slightly protruding from the vessel, I touched its flattened surface to the center of my bottom lip. Standing on my tippy toes to see my mouth in the mirror, I rubbed my lips together and then formed them into a heavy pout. I reached for a tissue quickly as I heard Nonna yelling from the next room to return with her tweezers. Scrubbing my face side to side with dry tissue, bits of white fibers balled up on my lips as I cleaned the evidence off my face. Snatching the tweezers from the corner of the cabinet where they have stood since the house had been built, I ran back to the kitchen to help Nonna with the cheek hair and the baccala.

CHAPTER 9

$\mathcal{D}$ay thirty-seven passed, and day thirty-eight arrived in my parents' house. Sitting on the edge of the single bed in the tight room, I looked at my feet. My toenails had grown ragged and looked primal. Rising from the edge of the bed, I made my way to the bathroom down the hall. Pulling open the drawer, I reached for the nail clippers and walked to the edge of the bathtub. I lowered myself onto the cold edge of the tub and leaned forward, pressing my entire body weight into my knees. There was hesitation with the clippers in my hand, my toes flexed and awaiting treatment.

"If you clip your nails, Annalise, this is it," I told myself, the words the tiniest whisper from my lips.

My hand that held the clippers began to tremble, the other hand squeezing my foot tight, preparing myself. I clipped each nail as short as it would go, gently as I could. My hands steadied with each movement, and I examined the fresh band of skin revealed at the edge of each digit. The skin so pink and tender looking, having not seen daylight or touched the air or been exposed to life yet. Leaving the clippings gathered onto the floor once I finished both feet, I used my pointer finger like a push broom and stacked the nails into a mound on the linoleum tile. I pinched the nails between my finger and thumb and gathered them in the palm of my hand. Walking to the counter, I placed the clippers back into the drawer and reached for a single square of toilet paper, laying it next to the sink and placing the clippings into the center. Carefully, I folded each edge over the pile until a small envelope formed, securing the discarded nails.

"That's it," I told my reflection, looking directly into the mirror.

My face was not recognizable; my hair so flattened to my head, and my eyebrows had grown unruly. I reached my fingers to my forehead and felt the line that now settled between my eyes. Walking back to the tub, I reached for the faucet, turning the water as hot as it could go, and set the drain stopper. I stared into the water filling the tub with force; it was murky in color from the pressure.

After sliding out of my clothes, I stepped into the bath, feeling the scalding water envelop my foot, my ankle burning with the pain of the temperature. I didn't care; I stepped my other leg over the edge and plunged my body into the fervid pool. Sliding down on my back, I let the water cover my head, my ears, and my face as I squeezed my eyes tightly shut. Running my nails over my scalp slowly, I blew the air out through my nose, allowing the bubbles to escape rapidly. Holding my breath until the burning became unbearable, I lifted my mouth just above the surface. I opened my lips to let the air in, and relief rushed through my body. I kept my body as still as I could in the bathtub in my parent's house until the water went cold and I began to shiver.

I flicked the drain plug out with my toe and watched the water get sucked down into a tornado at the end of the tub. Drying off, I wrapped the towel tightly under my arm and combed my hair while staring at my reflection. I looked at my arms, and then glanced down at my legs and tried to imagine Dylan's tattoos covering my body. Balancing the brush on the edge of the sink, I pinched the skin on my forearm, leaving a white spot behind after I released it. I leaned in close to the mirror and examined my lower lip; I studied the tiny spot on the inside of my lip where I had broken the skin at Dr. Fletcher's office a few days before. The swelling had gone away, only a faint hint of red remaining in its place as evidence.

I tightened the towel more securely under my arm and reached for the tiny tissue pillow filled with nail clippings. Clasping my fingers around it, I felt a small sharp nail poke through into my palm. I squeezed it harder and turned back to my room to find clean clothes.

CHAPTER 10

*R*unning my fingers down the fine mesh of the screen door at our back porch, I stood in hesitation, spotting, in the corner of the wooden frame, a delicate spider web that would be ruined when I pulled the door back to enter. Lurching the screen toward myself, I reached for the door handle to the main wooden entry, like I had so many times before. The door opened, and I stepped onto the hardwood in the kitchen. I awaited the familiar sound of the boards adjusting beneath my feet. I set my keys on the table and walked to the kitchen window over the sink, then leaned forward to look around. The mixing bowl I'd left outside weeks earlier, overturned on the ground next to the dead fig tree, was covered in specks of grass from the neighbor's lawn being mowed.

Wandering cautiously to the living room, I stood in front of my reading chair. My eyes hung on a small stain on the arm of the chair where my coffee had spilled over. Walking to the chair, I sat down, pulling my feet up under me. I stared into the room, noticing how the space had been untouched since I was last here. A plate sat on the floor next to the chair, riddled with crumbs from eating toast.

There was a pair of socks next to the couch that Dylan had discarded one night after work, likely while reading his book, still open to where he'd left off and lying face down on the cushion at the edge of the sofa. *Zen and the Art of Motorcycle Maintenance*, a book he'd read many times before. I reached for the paperback and examined the cover, barely hanging on to the binding, the corners creased, and the text worn away. Reading the title again, and under it, the author had captioned it *An Inquiry into Values*.

Running my fingers over the text, I felt what was left of the subtle embossing in the font nearly rubbed smooth. Turning the book to the page he'd left on, I saw red pencil markings throughout the page. He'd underlined sections and circled thoughts; he'd added his own comments in the margins and scribbled them out. He loved this book; it was his manifesto. After reading it for the first time with raw excitement, he told me that it had been written for him— stopping every few sentences to read the thought aloud to me. My eyes fell on a sentence circled and underlined near the bottom of the page that read, "*The place to improve the world is first in one's own heart and head and hands, and then work outward from there.*"

I turned the book and opened it to the first page. I'd never read the book before, as Dylan relayed every detail to the point I felt like I already knew its contents. The title appeared in bold typeface again, and underneath the text, the author offered a sweeping thought on his writings: "*it should in no way be associated with that great body of factual information relating to orthodox Zen Buddhist practice. It's not very factual on motorcycles, either.*" I smiled at this line, hearing it read to me in Dylan's voice. Closing the book, I pinched it tightly in my hand at my side.

Walking over to the corner of the living room, I arrived at where his drawing desk stood in preservation. Above the desk covering the walls on both sides were layers of translucent tracing paper covered in red penciled sketches and stencils—the layers of drawings like scales on the back of a serpent overlapping at each side. I reached out to the drawings and ran my hand against the direction in which they hung, causing them to flutter and dance as they left my grasp. A flipbook of images flashed by; designs of peonies, dragons, snakes, skulls, hearts, roses, and names written in tightly coiled scripture. Women's faces graced the walls, their eyes all wide and bold with crowns of flowers in their hair.

There were drawings of mythical creatures and Gods, a large drawing of a kitsune overlapping many of the other stencils and sketches.

Kitsune was the Japanese word for fox, and was a creature Dylan loved drawing, and moreover, worshiped it as a tattoo. The kitsune has been believed to possess magical traits that grew stronger with age and wisdom; they could shape-shift to human forms and trick others around them. They were often faithfully drawn, strong as friends, lovers, and keepers of others, transformed by entering bodies and taking control of human vessels. I reached for the rendering of kitsune and pulled it free of its pin with a swift tug.

Setting down the book, I held the paper delicately from both edges, letting the light come through the back of the page. This kitsune had three tails; the more tails one had, the stronger and wiser they were said to be. I turned the page at an angle and imagined where Dylan would have placed this drawing on the body, the flow of the lines creating a figure eight with movement escaping from the creased page. I could picture it running down the length of a hip and wrapping around the thigh, the tails crossing over in front of the knee and tucking around the body.

Taking the drawing over to the mirror that hung in the narrow hallway, I set it on the floor. I quickly shuffled out of my leggings and discarded them onto the floor as I reached for the stencil paper, turning the kitsune until it fit the line of my fleshy hip as if it had been drawn for me. I smoothed the paper until it released the tension from its surface and conformed to the curve of my thigh. Looking up at my reflection in the mirror, I tilted my head to make the kitsune look me in the eye, and I held its attention carefully.

Shapeshifter. The fox clung to my person, and I saw him in the reflection, in my face, and in my hands in the mirror. Feeling the power of his possession seep over my body, he took on my intentions, my mind, my hurt. The transmorpher had taken control and had burned the lines of the drawing into my leg where I held the paper. I pulled the drawing away from my skin, walked back to the living room, and set it in the center of the floor, turned at an angle to mimic its placement on my hip. My neck and face were stippled with sweat, and I stared down into the eyes of the witch animal that had wrapped its tails around my heart.

Gliding back to the drawings in my stocking feet and bare legs, I walked around the back of the desk. I noticed pencil shavings and eraser debris scattered all over the desktop; I constantly asked Dylan to clean this up as it stuck to his beard and clothing and speckled the house. Reaching out, I swept the drawing crumbs onto the floor carelessly, looking at my palm and examining the red streaks on my knuckles and the pads of my fingers. Rubbing my bare thigh with my hand to diffuse the color, I leaned over to the drawings once again.

Starting on the far-left side, I methodically lifted each sheath of paper, each and every design, drawing, rendering, gestural sketch, and finished tattoo stencil. I thought of the hours he'd spent craning over the desk with discarded sketches on the floor tossed to each side, thinking of each client wearing this permanent badge laid by Dylan's hand and drilled into their flesh with ceremony.

My hands stopped on a drawing of a large, long bird with its wings stretching across the page. It was a heron. Pulling her from the wall, I held her up to the light, watching the life in her gaze as she held my attention. Cherry blossoms fell around her, trickling down the stencil in perfect detail and symmetry. I pulled my sweater over my head and rushed back to the mirror with the bird goddess clutched tightly to my chest. I turned her to face my reflection, walking toward my body in a powerful march. Her strong body spread across my chest, grasping each shoulder and creating movement with her wings.

"Be the heron," I heard my bookstore muse whisper. I glanced back over to the kitsune on the floor and felt myself embodying the spirit of the clandestine fox. I pulled the tracing paper from my chest and rushed to the floor, lurching down onto my knees in front of the kitsune. I offered him the drawing of the heron in flight, and placed it above, where my chest would sit in relation to my hip and thigh.

I sat back onto my heels, my fleshy belly folding over the top of my underwear. I exhaled heavily, forcing all the air from my lungs, causing the kitsune to flutter gently from the escaping wind. I knew what the kitsune intended for me, and the shapeshifter curated my movements. Feeling my heart beating rapidly, I ran back to the wall feverishly, knowing what image I needed to find. Kitsune forced my hands through the drawings roughly, tearing drawings off the wall one by one and discarding them onto the floor. Underneath the layers lived the deity I was searching for, his image drawn in my mind. Catching a glimpse of an elephant's trunk, I stopped; I had found what kitsune was casting for. Beneath a neatly drawn bouquet of daisies, I could see the hazy figure taking shape, the Ganesha, looked back at me.

Reaching under the blanket of designs, I grabbed the corner of the page and freed him from the wall. The worshiped Hindu figure sat proudly in the center of the page, the head of an elephant, sitting cross-legged upon a throne, his ankles coiled in sacred thread. Clutching the deity, I ran to the mirror, my heart filling my chest. Holding the Ganesha onto my opposite thigh, I gazed down at the flowing lines forming the powerful body. The Ganesha required worship and commanded power and recognition in every culture. The remover of obstacles and an orator of intellect and wisdom. The powerful god stood for new beginnings and had the power to bring people together. He stared across my body from the temple of my leg and looked over to my other thigh where the lines of kitsune had laid claim.

Reaching for my leggings, I scrambled to pull them back on, my foot continually getting stuck on its way in.

I crawled under the drawing table amongst the discarded drawings and searched for my sweater. Pulling it over my head, trying to force both arms in at once, it caught on my hair pulled back into a loose bun. I knelt and placed the kitsune in front of me, carefully setting the swooping heron next, with Ganesha atop the pile. Turning the drawings, I began to roll them into a safe tubular shape; once rolled into place, I found a small black elastic on the drawing table, which at one time likely held a money roll firmly in Dylan's pocket. I rolled the elastic over the drawings until they were safely bound, let the cylinder slide down my hand, grabbed *Zen and the Art of Motorcycle Maintenance,* and ran to the door carrying the rolled stencils at my side like a sword.

CHAPTER 11

I laid awake that night in my childhood bed, but no tears came to my eyes. My mind had cleared a tiny spot from the foggy window, and I could gaze out and see shapes. I watched the glowing plastic stars until they lost their last bit of luster and turned into dull plastic shapes on the ceiling, having released all their stored energy from the day prior. Stretching across the bed, I reached to pull the small metal beaded chain to turn on the wooden bedside lamp with a taupe shade. The sound of the chain pulling the switch to turn the light on echoed in my ears, and the bright burning bulb filled the room.

I pulled Dylan's paperback novel off the side table. Sitting next to it lived the small tissue pillow containing my nail clippings from days before. I opened the book somewhere in the middle.

My brain clung to the lines Dylan had marked in red pencil, and I read aloud the small thought in the center of the left page. "*Who really can face the future? All you can do is project from the past, even when the past shows that such projects are often wrong. And who really can forget the past? What else is there to know?"* My hands shook slightly; I read on. *"You look at where you're going and where you are and it never makes much sense, but then you look back at where you've been and a pattern seems to emerge. And if you project forward from that pattern, then sometimes you can come up with something."* I closed the book quickly, leaving my finger in place to save the page.

Resting the book on my chest, I watched it move up and down slowly with my lungs. Folding up the bottom corner of the page without looking down, I wrapped both hands tightly around the small volume. I laid like this for some time, until my window brightened with sunlight. The kitsune inside of me began to stir, and I looked over to the roll of drawings sitting proudly on the edge of the dresser like Excalibur, calling to be pulled from the stone.

Springing up, I dashed to the closet, doors open and clothing spilling into a pile at my feet. Wading through the pile, I found clean jeans and Dylan's Guns n' Roses t-shirt, along with a hoodie with the tattoo shop's logo printed across the back. I shoved a few more items and Dylan's book into a small backpack leaning in the corner, and reached for a stiff cardboard tube laying on the shelf in the closet containing a poster rolled tightly from a museum exhibition I'd visited on a school field trip in fourth grade. Pulling off the cap, I shook it violently until the end of the poster peeked out. I reached for the glossy paper, pulled it free of the tube, and discarded it onto the floor. Gently, I placed the tattoo stencils wrapped with the kitsune as their keeper into the tube and replaced the cap on the end. Pulling on heavy socks and a pair of combat boots that zipped up the side,

I took a step to the mirror and glanced at my reflection. The darkened circles around my eyes were pronounced, the thin skin barely concealing the blood running beneath the surface. I clasped the backpack's buckle and headed for the stairs.

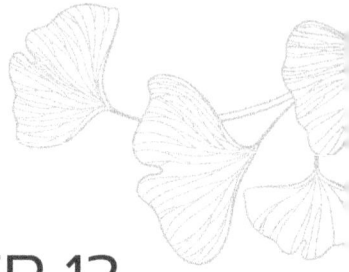

CHAPTER 12

*S*tanding at the end of the rough driveway, I examined the weeds forcing their way through the cracked cement; leaves were gathered in a corner, swept together by the nightly winds. I appraised the door to the right side of the garage, evaluating the number of steps it would take to reach the metal door. Maybe twelve. Stepping toward the garage slowly, I floated to the door, clutching my fingers tightly around the cardboard transport tube at my side. My head felt light, and the heavy combat boots demanded effort with each step. Reaching for the door with the dirty glass window, I peered through.

I searched the darkened chamber for the boots turning in my line of vision, but it was clear. My fingers pulsed as I reached for the handle. Turning the knob, I bumped my hip into the center of the door to release it from the tight and swollen frame; it opened, and I stepped one foot into the low space. Pins and needles surged to my hands, and my arms became stiff columns as I tentatively crept over to the Harley in its resting place. I walked to the side of the bike and ran my hand over the tank, taking a thin layer of dust with me. I pulled the backpack from my shoulders, let it slip down my arm onto the floor, and softly placed the cardboard tube next to the bike.

Reaching for the handlebars, I tried to straighten the bike from its resting position, but it didn't budge. Leaning further over the tank, I pulled as hard as I could, still nothing. I fumbled in my pocket for the small chrome-colored key and wiggled it into the steering column beside the tree with ease. Pressing my weight down into the key, it turned, while guiding the handlebars to the right; I'd seen Dylan do this so many times before, but I surprised myself when I released the lock so easily, feeling a tinge of confidence surge into my fingers. I swung my leg over the bike, careful to avoid the sissy bar sticking up proudly off the back fender. My foot landed with a hard thud on the cold cement as I gripped the bars tightly and pulled the bike straight, surprised by its weight on tilt. Digging my heels into the garage floor, I squeezed the grips as hard as I could, examining the dash, gauges, cables, and lights in front of me.

I looked on the left side of the bike and found the hand clutch lever attached to the handlebar, just like the dirt bike I had ridden as a kid around my parents' cabin, on the logging roads with my cousins, in the final light of a summer's evening. Grasping the lever, I imagined releasing the power from the rear wheel to shift gears. I ran my fingernail over the fine grooves in the handlebar grip, allowing my nail to skip over the texture, making a dull and repetitive noise as if playing a tiny instrument.

I felt with my toe for the shifter, clumsily kicking back and forth with my boot until settling on the metal and practicing the motion of my hand and foot working together to switch gears. Nervousness warmed my body, remembering how I used to pop out the clutch and jerking forward on my old childhood dirt bike. *Would I be strong enough to manage this bike*, I thought.

Reaching over to the right side of the bike, I examined the throttle and handbrake attached to the handlebar; my eyes followed the brake cable down the fork to where it attached to the front wheel. Glancing back behind me, I looked down for the lever to control the rear brake, mimicking this action with my toe and heel. I thought of my dad taking me out to the industrial park to practice driving for the first time in his old Volkswagen Jetta with the standard transmission, lurching the old navy blue box forward and stalling the engine over and over again. Running through the order of engaging the bike in my mind, I started up the motor, revving the engine and gradually releasing the clutch to cautiously transition into gear. Pulling in the clutch lever and forcing my foot down onto the gear shift, I pushed down several times until the resistance stopped under my foot. The bike felt heavy in my grip, fatigue setting in and causing shaking as my arms reached up to the exaggerated handlebars.

Digging my feet firmly into the ground, I reached out with hesitation to turn the key; the engine coughed, then cleared its throat, then fired up with a full and deep vibration rumbling in my ears. I felt my body tingling. Putting the bike into neutral with my toe, I pulled up hard and clumsily. I sat very still, allowing the bike to vibrate through me, feeling the power of the engine begging to be released, and numb the inside of my thighs where they rested at the sides of the bike. Pressing my tongue to the roof of my mouth, I clenched my back teeth down. Squeezing my eyes shut as tightly as I could, I fought to keep Dylan's face out of my mind; I was afraid of him seeing me on his prized motorcycle without permission. I tensed as if he would walk through the garage door and catch me.

Eventually, my body relaxed, and the bike didn't seem so heavy. I don't know how long I sat there, the fumes from the exhaust filling my nose and mouth. Reaching my foot back, I felt for the kickstand and flexed it forward until it became engaged. I rested the bike to its side, feeling it settle onto the stand and give over its weight to the sturdy peg. Sliding my leg off the bike, I balanced on one foot carefully as not to touch the tank with my boot.

I moved to the garage door and crouched to reach for the tattered yellow rope, frayed and secured to the center of the door. Giving it a strong tug as I stood up, I released it from its resting place on the dirty, uneven cement. Pushing it overhead using both hands, I felt my muscles stretching as I lifted onto my tiptoes to settle the door open overhead. I shuffled to the workbench in the shop and reached for Dylan's crumpled leather jacket where he'd left it. Putting it on, I noticed the dust that had collected on the shoulder. The sleeves were long, and after I zipped it up, there was a gap at the back where a man's frame should have filled it out. Lifting my arms in the air to force the jacket down, I pinched them to my body to hold it in place.

I reached for his helmet, running my hands over the root-beer-colored metal flake revealing the brilliant twinkle as the domed surface caught the light. Pulling it tight down over my head, I secured the strap under my chin with shaking hands. Reaching for my backpack, I secured it onto my shoulders, grabbed the cardboard tube, and walked back to the bike; I stepped around to the front of the bike and pulled at the bungee cord that tied down a Mexican serape blanket across the bottom of the handlebars, rolled tight into a cylinder. Releasing the brightly striped fabric onto the floor with the flick of my wrists, I laid the tube of drawings at one end. I inched the fabric around the stencils until it fit into a tight coil and reattached it to the front fork.

Climbing back onto the bike, I released the kickstand as I stood the weighty metal frame back into position. Pressing my toes into the ground, I looked over my shoulder, swinging with momentum to lurch the bike backward; I began walking my feet slowly backward, wheeling the bike out of the garage and onto the alleyway. Laying into the throttle slightly, I felt the burp of the pipes jolt through my legs. Pulling the clutch lever in to disengage the rear wheel, I pushed down my left foot to put the bike into first gear. I pulled the throttle and eased my hand off of the clutch; the bike jumped forward and jerked, but I steadied it quickly and calmed my hand on the throttle as the motor climbed. Hooking my toe under the shifter, I popped it into second gear with another clumsy lurch forward, the motor dampening between gears. My heart pounded in my ears, held tightly by the helmet; I could feel the sweat heating up my visor, and I exhaled a long, slow breath through my pursed lips.

What are you doing, Annalise? I mouthed to myself, glancing down at the teardrop shape of the tank between my legs, running my eyes over the unfamiliar gauges and dials between the bars. "What are you doing?" I shouted at the top of my lungs, my throat straining in pain.

Pulling in the clutch, I laid off the throttle and slid the bike into third with a softer touch, easing off the clutch smoothly, reducing the jarring. Feathering the throttle, I massaged the gears. I thought about a line that stuck with me from *Zen and the Art of Motorcycle Maintenance*: *"Your common sense is nothing more than the voices of thousands and thousands of these ghosts from the past."* The ghost of Dylan was sitting on my chest; I forced all his weight into me, depressing my breathing, slowing my heart, and pinching his fingers at the base of my nervous system. Carrying the ghost of my Nonna on my back, I held my hair from my eyes, whispering to me in her thick accent, *"Bambina, ghosts are no real. You are real."*

Pulling back hard on the throttle, I let the pipes crack as loud as I forced them to go, tightening my grip as Dylan tried to throw me off the bike.

I dug in.

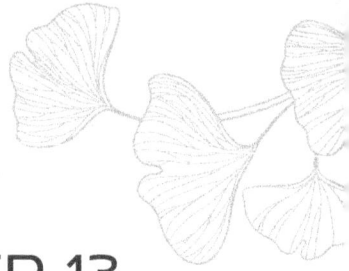

CHAPTER 13

I didn't know where I was going, just that I needed to go away. My arms were numbed from the handlebar position, and the vibration of the rough pavement massaged my body as I slowly gained confidence in controlling the bike. I instinctually headed to The Easel; my movements guided by habit, making the turns to the store as if automated on a rail. Clinging to the bike, nerves surged through my body. The bike was much bigger than anything I'd ridden, and I became cautiously aware of its weight below me. We were yet to establish trust.

As I approached the front door to the store, I dropped my feet off the pegs and allowed them to brush the pavement to steady me as I coasted to a stop. I pushed the bike onto its kickstand, this time with ease. Leaving the bike running, I hopped across the sidewalk to the store's front door. I raced inside, my feet slipping on the smoothly worn tiles. I pushed past the patrons craning over the tables and hovering near the shelves. At the back of the store, I fell quickly to my knees and dug my arm, clad in Dylan's jacket, to the back of the shelf and felt for my book. My hand instantly recognized its thick and powerful shape. Pulling it into the light on the floor in a single movement, I stopped my fingers on the marked page.

Fudo Myo-o. I steadied my fingers and lightly tugged the page free, starting at the top from its binding. The finely tattered edge released from the heavy stitching and glue with much less resistance than I expected. I turned the book to the dust cover and looked at the small dotted image of Horiyoshi, once more staring into his tiny features until he began to look like a fingerprint. Pushing myself onto my feet with the Fudo Myo-o in hand, I headed back outside to the bike, bumping a woman's shoulder at the door. "Sorry!" I called as I hurried past. My bike was where I'd left it, still purring in wait. I released the drawings from their safe nest on the front of the bike, hidden and padded in the blanket, and rolled the Fudo Myo-o around them as a protector and keeper; the glossy page felt substantial in my hands next to the tracing paper pieces. I refastened the tube in its hiding place and mounted the bike.

Finding myself idling at the edge of the Glenmerry Cemetery, I planted my feet on either side of the bike. I turned off the engine, released the chin strap from the helmet, and plucked it off my head. I hung it on the handlebar as I dismounted the bike and walked onto the nearest pathway to enter the grounds. The grass had started browning from the summer's heat, and a thick, strong clover sprouted up at the edges and forced its way through the cement. Kicking the top off a piece of the low, green plant, I walked to the end of the pathway. Turning down the second row, I came upon three tight headstones in a row together; the far right said *Salvidori Tossono*. Mr. Tossono, in his resting place where Carmina and I had left him over twenty years ago. Walking to his grave, smooth with brown grass, I stood square to face him. I lowered my body into a crouch, the stiffness of the leather jacket guiding my hands to the grass awkwardly.

"I was actually afraid of you," I found myself saying aloud to the headstone, carved of pink granite placed stoically into the ground.

Pushing myself back to my feet, I turned on my heel, feeling the weight on my combat boots in tow.

I felt each step as I walked to the opposite corner of the graveyard, the top left side near the chain-link fence. The property backed onto an elementary school, which never struck me as strange until now. Feeling myself being pulled like a magnet toward her, I glided over to the two stones side-by-side appearing at the crest of the property, tucked away. When I arrived at their graves, I stood exactly between the two for a moment respectfully, before moving in front of Nonna's grave.

Stepping forward with hesitation close to the stone, I felt torn about standing on the piece of earth which housed her body. Dropping down to my knees, I placed the palms of my hands flush onto the intricate stone. I felt the space between my fingers where the letters had been engraved, reading her name, her birth year, the year of her death, and the words, "*Sotto la mano di Dio*." It read, "Under God's hands."

Am I God right now? I thought to myself, embarrassed that my mind allowed for this thought. I felt the warmth of the sun captured in the stone; I spread my fingers apart as wide as they could go.

"Where are you, Nonna?" I asked the stone. Pressing with my fingertips, I could feel the fine layer of grit on the polished rock's surface. "I need you," I croaked through a tightened throat, my eyes blurred with the heat of tears.

"You're not with God, Nonna. God is not real. I am real; be with me," I begged of her, my shoulders heaving as relief began to wash over me after days of holding in this dull and enveloping pain.

"Help me. I want you to help me! You have to help me; you have to fix me. I will do better! I will be better, please, Nonna!" I wailed, my head slouching forward as I laid on my side and pulled my knees to my chest.

Waking to the rough grass pressing a fine and detailed pattern into my cheek, I scratched at the spot as it stung with a pleasant pain. I pulled a small leaf from the collar of the jacket and got up to my feet. Standing between the tombstones, I placed a hand on both Nonna and Nonno. I moved back in front of Nonna's resting place and licked my pointer finger. In the fine, dusty film on the surface of the stone, I drew a long teardrop-shaped tail, and then added one more on each side. The kitsune, with three tails in rough form like the walls in the caves of Lascaux. The shape-shifter was waiting for me at the street, wrapped tightly on the front of the bike, calling me to ride.

CHAPTER 14

I began to drive to the coast without any real direction. I just felt the pull to the west and began to ride. I felt much steadier on Dylan's large bike; the wobbles were gone, and my confidence improved even though I lacked a license. I didn't care.

After a few hours on the bike, my body ached deeply from the contorted position, and my newness to the stamina required to sit in the same rigid bend at length. Fatigue was setting in. My body was tense, clutching the handlebars. I was riding with caution and fear in my joints as I traveled down the highway in the slow traffic lane, trucks, trailers, and cars all flying past me.

Without turning my head, I moved my eyes toward the signage approaching at the side of the road and scanned for the gas symbol at the upcoming exits. *Exit 28* had gas and food; I extended my right hand down low to the side and pointed to the ground to signal my upcoming turn, as Dylan had stripped the bike of the signal lights. This caused me to let off the throttle, and the bike lurched and quickly wobbled. Feeling the adrenaline spring up, my face became flushed and hot, my body wracked with fear from riding without both hands clinging tightly to the bars. It reminded me that I was still a rookie.

Turning into the gas station, I slowly approached the closest pump and dismounted the bike. My arms and legs were numb, my hands and wrists cramped and pulsing, my backside aching, and my lower back felt stiff and sore. I dug my thumbs into my spine and leaned back while tilting my head up.

Dylan had ridden this road many times; he ventured to the coast and followed the curves of the ocean and the gnarled switchbacks of the cliffs every year. He never invited me to join him, no matter how many times I had hinted that I wanted to see the same edges and ride along with him.

I released the gas cap from the tank and nervously shifted my eyes to the surrounding pumps in search of a fellow rider. I didn't want to be noticed, look novice, or seem out of place with the bike, but my movements were awkward, and I felt embarrassed. There was only one other vehicle near me, an older minivan, dull steel in color and full of a family who paid me no mind. I left my helmet on intentionally and tucked my hair up under the back to create the illusion of androgyny.

With the tank refueled, I took large and purposeful strides across the parking lot to the attendant's door. I grabbed a few snack bars, water, and a map labeled *Pacific Coast Highway 1*. It had been a decade or more since I'd read a paper map, but Dylan always had one while on his bike; there were often parts of the journey without cell service, no fellow riders, and no way to call home.

"Hey, do you know where I can find a surplus store around here?" I questioned the frumpy and unshaven man behind the counter.

He didn't look up, just tilted his head to the highway and said, "Yup, twenty minutes or so down the road, you'll see the sign. They also got firecrackers." I stared down at his worn knuckles, fine rims of black grease lining each nail bed.

"Thanks," I nodded, scooping my items off the counter and jogging to the bike. I nestled the supplies into the bag, aside from the map, which I folded and tucked into my jacket.

Reaching inside the backpack, I felt for my passport and a money roll where I had hidden them between the lining and the main body of the bag. I mounted the bike and followed the signs to a roadside surplus store right on the edge of the Washington border. Rushing through the musty, temporary attraction, I grabbed a small tent in army green, a tarp, sleeping bag, a few pieces of cookware, flashlight, batteries, sleeping mat, matches, fuel in a tiny canister, a package of bungee cords, and a stuff sack.

After I paid for the items, I rushed outside and pulled all the tags off the gear, shoving them tightly into the camo-print-covered sack, and strapped them to the sissy bar with the bungee cords. I attached the tent on top of it all and pulled at it with both hands to ensure it felt secure.

Good enough.

I pulled the map from inside my coat and released it from its perfectly folded resting position. Holding this paper map and examining the routes made me feel legitimate, like a real rider on a solo adventure.

I found my approximate location sitting on the border just East of Washington state. Crouching down on the ground, I spread the map in front of me. Sitting on my knees, I leaned over it tightly and examined the tangled system of roads before me. I traced my finger across the mint green surface and followed an artery that took me to the edge of the ocean, my eyes searching for the legend to see how many miles this leg would take.

Springing up, I dug for my phone in the side pouch, checking the time. One minute before 11 a.m. I had all day to cross the state, ride south, and settle in before dark. I glanced back down at the map, the side lifting in the light breeze. I bent over and picked it up by the corner and folded it back into its rightful position, and tucked it inside Dylan's coat. Zipping the jacket all the way to the top, I pulled on my glasses and gloves, and ensured my braid was fully secured up under the helmet.

I was going to do this.

CHAPTER 15

The roads got smaller, and the traffic lightened as I neared the coastline. Deep shadows from age-old growth surrounded the road ahead of me, tricking my eyes over and over. Searching for the white line to guide me on my right, I clenched the handlebars tightly until my fingers were void of feeling. I forced myself to relax and trust the bike. I searched ahead with each curve of the road, looking for the green signs telling me how far until my destination, riding along the highway nearing the water. Seeing a sign up ahead, *Astoria, 13 miles*, I felt relief.

I would cross the border to Oregon, ride south on its coast, and rest for the night before hitting California. I pulled slowly into traffic nearing the junction and saw the sprawling Columbia River appear to my left, textured with waves and its powerful current pushing toward the mouth, begging to be released into the ocean. My eyes followed the river to the massive bridge before me, the Astoria-Melger Bridge—the connection to Highway 101, a proud and dominant cantilever steel structure fearlessly spanning the four-mile gap between the masses of earth. I felt my pulse racing and sweat collecting around my face as I approached the bridge entrance.

My Nonno had told me stories of this bridge. It's made from steel in the plant where he worked for forty years, along with my father and even his Nonno before him. They had arrived on a boat from the old country to labor here, working with their hands and smelting metals for buildings, bridges, and infrastructure across the western states and Canadian provinces. He told me how the bridge had been constructed in sections and floated ninety miles down the river. They were hoisted from barges and positioned into place by armies of workers, each one leaving their mark on this conduit.

He spoke of the bridge as if he'd built it himself, though he had no way of knowing if his labor had been intertwined in this structure; I suspected all the men laid claim to this bridge when telling the story to their families and children of its coming together. It was part of the legend of the men that labored for generations to build the state.

Pedestrians were not allowed to cross the bridge. It was reserved for motorists and bikes only, but one day a year, in October, the Great Columbia Bridge Crossing was hosted. The spanning structure became open for foot traffic to run a race. My Nonno always talked about going to run this race, though he'd never owned a pair of running shoes, and I'd never seen him exert himself in the way of intentional exercise before. I smiled at the memory of him telling me the story of the bridge, and it settled my nerves as I approached the steep entrance to the span. I looked down as my front tire crossed the pavement over a metal strap that marked the start of the structure; the slightly grooved surface pulled my tires in a small pattern toward the rail, and I clutched tightly to control the steering. My heart raced, and I could feel every vein light up in my body. I gazed over the side quickly and saw the water rushing against the pattern of the bridge deck. I then approached the crest of the structure and felt a swell of pride filling my body.

As I descended the other side of the bridge and entered back onto the road, I looked up and saw a large sign overhead, it read *Astoria 101*, with a graphic of the Oregon grape, the state's flower, illustrated below in a single-colored yellow print.

Turning down the first side road, I found a coffee shop on my right with single metal tables littering a nearly empty patio. I parked the bike out front, hung my helmet, grabbed my backpack, and headed inside.

After settling outside with a small hot cup of black coffee, I reached for the map from my pocket, spreading it out on the table before me. It was much larger than the surface and hung over the edges in every direction.

I moved my coffee onto the chair next to me to make room. Finding Astoria, I examined the text on the page as if it were going to tell me a secret. Looking around the modest patio space, I found the side table where the servers left menus and discarded dishes. I took a pen from the tabletop assortment and circled Astoria, the pen skipping along the fine grate of the perforated table below. I lightened my pressure and circled it multiple times until the lazy oval jumped off the page.

Scanning the coastline, I mouthed the names of the upcoming towns that followed the 101: Seaside, Lincoln

City, Newport. I began trying to memorize the order in which the towns appeared. As I studied the upcoming route and planned my stops for gas and food, I noticed a shadow creeping over the side of the page. Glancing to my right, I saw the arm of a denim jacket, dirtied on the cuff, hanging beside my shoulder.

"Hello," I said with some hesitation, turning my torso on the cold seat to face the person.

"Hi, Girly," the man bellowed in a slow and measured baritone. "Jim," he stated factually as he reached his thick hand out to me. It enveloped mine and shook it firm with two deliberate pumps.

"Annalise," I nodded, looking down at my body and feeling embarrassed wearing Dylan's jacket.

"Your baby?" he gestured with his chin over to Dylan's bike leaning on its kickstand on the other side of the patio railing.

"Uh, um, yeah. Sort of, yes. I rode it here, yeah," I fumbled, trying to convince Jim, and trying to convince myself.

"Well, ya made it a decent distance," he offered, looking at the headlight speckled with bugs and flecks of dirt.

I'm fooling him, I thought, shifting my weight in the chair to the opposite hip.

"Mind if I sit?" Jim questioned and reached for the chair next to me before I could respond.

He had a black patterned bandana tied around his neck, poking out of the top of his heavily worn denim jacket. The bandana had settled into perfectly uniform rings after years of wear. The jacket looked thick, lined with fleece, a touch of brown corduroy folding over at the collar. A tiny patch no bigger than a postage stamp was stitched onto the breast pocket, a finely embroidered image of the head of a sable-colored German Shepard. The other side had a patch that read "Ass, Grass, or Cash, no one rides for free," bordered with a green rectangle of stitching. He had a smooth grey mane pulled into a low ponytail at the nape of his neck, and a long silky matching beard with the mustache covering his mouth.

"So, where you headin'?" Jim asked with ease. Bikes attracted fellow bikers, so I had to fake this part until I understood my place. I felt nervous and fraudulent and excited to be invited in.

"I'm not totally sure," I offered with honesty. "I'm heading to the PCH, and I don't know after that." My gaze darted down to the map, the town of Astoria jumping back at me.

Jim nodded long and slow, digesting my plan, or lack thereof. "Who built the bike for you?" Jim nodded to the bike again on the street. I wasn't prepared for this question. *I stole it*, I thought, but I couldn't say that.

"It is my husband's. It was my husband's; it's mine now. He built it." The words came out choppy; I felt guilty saying it.

"It's a beauty," Jim offered, brushing over my comment about who the bike belonged to. "Someone knew what they were doing when they put her together."

I nodded, examining the machine.

The lines of the bike were low, sloping slowly toward the ground at the rear. The minimal handlebars and parsed-down finishes stood strong. The tobacco-colored leather of the single seat held worn lines and shapes from miles of use.

The sissy bar stuck proud off the back, loaded haphazardly with my gear strapped onto it. The pipes were wrapped in fine mesh, the flat paint intentionally without shine absorbed light from around it.

"'81?" Jim asked.

"'83," I answered confidently. I could remember that, the year I'd been born.

"Don't see many Shovelheads around no more. I had a '76 a long time ago; she had a ton of problems. Drank oil and had a big 'ol engine knock. I loved that girl, but she never quite loved me back," a smile lit the corners of his eyes as if he were talking about a former lover.

I nodded vigorously, pretending to follow his comments. "Yeah, Dylan spent a lot of time working on this bike. She broke down on him often, but he'd never have traded her in for something more reliable. He had grit—often too much."

"You see those lines there?" Jim extended his pointer finger, tracing the shape of the engine in the air. "Them are two turned-around coal shovels; looks just like 'em. Ten more horsepower in that girl, she can dance," he said with a chuckle, leaning the chair onto its back legs. "A lot of bike for you, but I know you have her figured out."

Jim's words provided relief, but I didn't believe it yet.

"Keep the oil topped up, kiddo. Every stop, top it off," his experienced tone resonated.

I thought back to the day on the road, knowing I hadn't given the oil a thought. "Jim, I've never checked the oil before, if I'm being honest. Can you show me where that is?"

What did I have to lose? I figured I'd just ask him and spare myself the embarrassment of a roadside rescue.

"Of course, honey," Jim smiled, almost waiting for the request. He pushed himself from the seat as I folded the map and tucked it safely back into my jacket.

We stood in front of the bike and Jim reached out, placing his hand on the tank. He gently ran the curve of metal. "This one's tricky, kiddo. You have to work a little magic, but nothing you can't handle, I figure." I raced my eyes all over the bike, trying to determine how to approach the project.

"Step over the bike and hold it up straight. Get it off the kickstand."

I obliged immediately, swinging my leg over the seat and jerking the bike straight as steady and quickly as I could.

"This one has a trap door of sorts. A couple steps, but you will follow."

I leaned over to watch Jim as he ran his hand along the underside edge of the seat.

He pulled free a small allen key, holding it up for me to see. "Got it," he smirked. "Same spot I stash mine." He knelt in front of the transmission and inserted the key into the cap on top. He twisted it slowly, letting a quiet whistle out through his teeth and bearded lips.

"A good rule of thumb with this old shovel is you don't need to check yer oil, you need to top up yer oil. No sense in fooling around." He pulled the cap from the top of the transmission and held it up to me like a Cracker Jack prize. I reached out and grabbed the cap, holding it tightly in the crease on my hand.

"Wait here," Jim ordered, pushing off his knee and taking long heavy strides across the street. He walked up to a Harley and pulled a quart of oil from the saddlebag, wrapping his large hand around it. He jogged back to where I still held the bike straight. "Now, this is a straight 60W," Jim informed me, facing the dirtied label to my gaze. "Some guys are old school, it's 80W all the way, but 60W will do you just fine heading south here."

I nodded, making a mental note.

"It's your bike, so you run the juice however you want, but 60W is a good start."

"Okay," I replied quietly, watching intently as he toggled the quart back and forth, sloshing the heavy fluid around inside.

"Just pour it straight in. That's how you check the oil in a shovel; it always needs some," he instructed, looking down at the fine drizzle of oil pouring into the engine. "When it runs out of the hole, you're done checking your oil. Just put that plug back in there, and you're good to go."

I watched as a golden burp of liquid brimmed at the opening. I reached out and offered the plug back to Jim, his rough hand grasping mine and plucking the cap from my palm.

He threaded it back in place with the allen key, wiping the excess oil in a swirl with his large pointer finger and cleaning it on his jeans. He snapped the allen key back into place under the edge of the leather seat and got to his feet.

"That's it, Girly." A wide grin covered his face and revealed yellowed bottom teeth fighting for space. "Top it up each stop, 'cause you'll burn it off as fast as you put it in!" he chuckled, shaking his head.

"Well, I'm off. You want to ride a bit with me or what?" looking back at his bike waiting across the street.

I sat onto the seat, pulling my helmet and gear on while he spoke. "Okay, Jim. But I have to tell you, I'm pretty new at riding, so I don't want to slow you down."

"I'm ancient, honey. You ain't gonna slow me down none," he nodded and crossed the street. I turned the key on the bike and felt the familiar shake of the pipes run through my legs, electricity filling my body.

Jim did a slow U-turn in the middle of the quiet side street that led us down to the intersection. My heart pounded in my ears over the rumble of the engine with its fresh oil. He rode with one hand on his thigh, tucked tightly into the fold of his hip. As soon as we entered the open road, traffic lightened. I kept my distance, watching his every move, following his long, deep, slow turns into each corner, trying to mimic the slope of his body and the simple grace of his leans.

I watched him extend his fingers on his left hand into a point down to the pavement whenever a fellow biker passed by, giving them the knowing signal wave—the secret handshake of the tribe that I now found myself in. I still felt too shy to try it, to release my grip, and to admit entrance to the club.

At times, Jim would fall back, riding the inside of the lane, his back tire aligned with my front tire moving in unison. We'd hold this pattern for miles, my cheeks numb from the wind and stinging with pain as bugs pelted me like tiny bullets. Jim reached into his collar with one hand and pulled the patterned bandana over his lips and nose, tucking his beard in and protecting his face from the shrapnel. Noted.

The sun had tracked overhead and moved toward its resting place near the ocean's horizon. I saw a sign that read *Bullards Beach State Park* just south of Coos Bay. I needed to pull in for the night, as much as I didn't want to leave Jim.

He looked over at me and, too nervous to take my hand off the handlebar, I nodded to the sign. Jim gave me one slow, steady nod and dropped his bike back so we were side-by-side without losing speed. He looked at me for a long time, ignoring the road ahead. He relied on me to guide us and keep us safe for these few fast moments. With a quick turn of the wrist, he pulled back hard on the throttle and the power of the bike lurched him forward. I heard the motor gaining speed as he released the clutch and shifted gears. He lowered his hand to the ground and pointed his fingers to the speeding pavement, giving me a brief goodbye wave. I felt a twinge of panic as his figure turned a corner and disappeared, the roar of his bike echoing across the ocean at my right.

I geared down into the turn and exited the main road into the state park.

CHAPTER 16

When I woke, the sky still shone black. No light passed through the darkened walls of my tent. The tent was still fresh with creases from being tucked into its pliable casing, and heavy with the scent of new plastic fibers. I sat up on my sleeping mat and reached for my toes, tilting my head side to side to loosen my neck, pain traveling into my shoulders from the stiff position of the Harley, which my body was not accustomed to.

I rubbed my deltoids with rough pressure and flexed my ankles back and forth to wake up each of the stiff joints.

What was I doing? I thought. I raised my hands in front of my face and examined the palms, turning them slowly to look at the rough and thin skin puckered across delicate bones. Feeling the burning in my knuckles from yesterday's ride, I flexed each digit then turned my palms to face in, lacing my fingers together and squeezing tightly.

What am I doing? I thought again. I crawled to the end of the tiny tent and felt for the stiff cardboard tube safely housing the drawings; my fingers clasped around the smooth cardboard shape and I pulled it to my chest. I pictured the elegant lines of the Fudo-Myo-o and asked the Acala god of wisdom to answer me. Picturing the noose in his left hand, outstretched toward me, I raised my hand to my throat, rubbing the skin unconsciously, my mind shooting to Dylan's feet visible in my eye-line when I entered the garage.

"Immovable Protector," I whispered, feeling foolish speaking to the paper tube in my hand. "Show me what to do, just show me what to do," I pleaded in the faintest croak of a voice. "Take my ghosts, take the evil spirits away as you promise. Protect me," I begged, pressing my mouth to the side of the tube, a dingy and familiar taste of pulp entering my system.

Squeezing my eyes tightly shut, I pictured the powerful deity binding my demons with the noose, holding them back from my reach. I opened my eyes and saw a hint of light forcing its way through the east side of my tent. Sitting back on my heels, I rested the cardboard tube across my thighs, a hand planted firmly on each end. I looked down at the case and saw a darkened wet print where my mouth had been, running my finger over the spot until the paper pilled under my touch.

Searching so hard will drain your system. You are hunting for love or for the taste of a memory that is no longer accurate, but you hold onto it so tightly that it will deplete you without warning. You grasp the other person's soul and look inside for a hint of the times that took away the pain, but all you can see is the pain itself reflected back at you. I set the tube aside and began gathering and packing my gear, preparing for the day's ride ahead.

It felt easier on the bike today, with no tension, no fear. Making my way back to Highway 101 on the southern edge of the Oregon Coast, the cedar trees grew with each mile underneath me. I'd driven this road before, as a young child about eight years old. I rode in the back seat of my Nonna and Nonno's chocolate brown Volvo station wagon with windows that only rolled halfway down to ensure no one jumped out. We were making a pilgrimage to Disneyland; myself, my older sister Janet, and Nonna and Nonno. It was a three-day drive from where we lived, and we'd stuck to the I5. Nonna talked Nonno into cutting across to the 101 for half a day through Oregon "so the-a girls can-a see the waters."

I'd never seen the ocean before that trip. Nonno pulled into a rest area packed with family vehicles, all stacked tall with bicycles, camp stoves, lawn chairs, and luggage strapped to roof racks. We parked the car, and Nonna yelled to us in the back seat, "roll up your windows, girl— the gypsies!" Always convinced that the rest of the world worked just like the old country and gypsies would rob you at any opportunity.

I wheeled the stiff, black handle furiously in the back-seat while my sister was already running to the edge of the parking lot to peer down at the ocean. I swung the car door open and pressed down the manual lock shaped like a golf tee before slamming it shut behind me. My toes squished with sweat inside of my translucent purple jelly shoes, speckled with glitter that my mother had bought me, for the trip. As I ran, a minuscule pebble flicked up into my shoe and stabbed me in the heel, but I didn't stop. I scrunched my foot and worked the pebble into the crease between my toes and the ball of my foot and held it in place while I dashed to the side of the lot next to Janet.

My breath felt tight and my tummy heaved, moving the light pink and white stripes across my belly as I worked to catch air. I studied the fine hair on the back of my hand and knuckles as it caught the light, surprised by its presence. I'd never noticed it before. Crouching down, I reached my finger into my jelly shoe and sifted for the pebble, flicking it free. I heard Nonna calling to us, "Girls! Girls! Careful at-a the water, you-a go down to the beach!" The staccato of her accent made the word beach sound like "bitch." Janet and I looked at each other and giggled at her swearing unintentionally. Janet pushed off ahead of me, charging toward the narrow path leading down to the beach. I followed as quickly as I could, feeling the sand bounce off my shins as I tucked in close behind her.

Running straight for the ocean's edge, we kicked and splashed at the white foam that gathered at the shoreline. It was flecked with pieces of kelp and mulch that had pushed its way to the beach. A set of small waves were rolling toward me, gathering speed and the slightest bit of height. When the first wave reached me, it touched my knees then swelled to wet the bottom hem of my shorts, changing them from bubble gum pink to deep fuchsia. I felt disoriented as if the ground were moving beneath me, and I turned away from the ocean and tried to scramble to shore.

It felt as if the earth had moved at lightning speed and the waves became a treadmill below. Falling to my knees, I clawed at the dense wet ground to push myself to the dry sand as panic encased my body. After a few feet, I was out of the waves and safely onshore. Nonna had made her way down the winding pathway by this time, standing over me, shaking her head and smiling.

"Bambina, what-a-matter-for-you?" she cooed through light-hearted laughter. I turned and glared back at the ocean, unsure as to what had happened, as it looked calm and inviting to the eye.

"I . . . I don't know Nonna. The ground, it moved!" I croaked, my voice quivering.

"The water no harm you, Bella. It-a show you where to go; just listen," she said, lowering herself into a slow squat to touch my head with her swollen fingertips. "No mind," she comforted as I looked back over my shoulder to see the shoreline flat and undisturbed.

CHAPTER 17

*I*found myself charging down the coastline, comfort settling in beneath me as I traced the patterns of the road in my mind. The highway narrowed and became pitted on the surface with long, steep descents arriving in deep switchbacks and returning to a crest with a short climb. The road undulated in this rhythm for hours on end, sweeping me up and down its snake-like body. Having left Oregon behind, the ride gathered intensity with each mile as California's terrain became exaggerated and difficult, but my body did not hesitate as I felt the pull south.

My belly started rumbling as I approached the small town of Point Reyes. Shifting the bike down as the pipes spat, I tried to conceal their volume as I slowly turned left onto Main Street. I pulled my bike up to the curb and parked it nose-in against the sidewalk, alongside a van without any windows in the back.

Leaving my helmet perched on the seat, I reached for my backpack and walked slowly past the shops of the town. Quaint storefronts, cafés, a barbershop, and a grocery co-op lined the street. Locals stopped to chat with their children running about, speckling the walkway. I approached the oak door standing before me, nestled into an alcove made of brick: Point Reyes Bookstore. It pulled me in, and the soft, familiar must filled my nostrils as a twinge of home dug into my side.

Pressing my heels into the floor with each step, I glided to the back wall, drawn by the overhead sign that read *Art & Photography*.

My eyes scanned the rows quickly, looking over the people sipping coffee and chatting, dotted throughout the store. I leaned in close to the shelf at my eye-line, letting my fingers skip across the spines. My eyes searched for *Crows and Herons*, but it was not here. My heart sank with the failure to find a glowing beacon telling me I was heading in the right direction. It wasn't there.

Crouching down, I rested onto the back of my boots; I scanned the shelves without purpose until my gaze landed upon a powder blue spine, bold text running toward the floor that read *Teddy Black: Tattooing the See-Through Man*. My stomach tightened at the sight of it. I reached in with a finger and tipped the book toward myself by the top of the spine, as if I were opening a doorway to a secret passage.

The cover depicted a man's silhouette, crowned in a fedora hat with bold rimmed glasses. His features were anonymous, and his posture proud. He pulled the buttons of his shirt apart wide to expose a center of light, revealing a contorted face of an alien or a lion, or both. A three-eyed creature that changed shape the longer I stared.

I flipped open the pages and scanned the full-scale color images that filled every corner of the paper. Teddy Black was a founding father of modern tattooing in American culture. I instantly recognized his imagery, bold lines, and saturated primary colors. Dylan had referenced him often; he was infatuated with him when he first began apprenticing a decade or more ago.

The book contained drawings, paintings, and the offering of skin as a canvas. It was a vector for his creations on display, transporting the mind to secret rooms, onto the floors of warm Japanese studios with artists crowded and hunching over their subjects with a Tabori tool in hand.

I turned each page, heavy with preservation in its quality, and examined the finely patterned lines and large blocks of color. When I arrived at the final graphical page, I turned to the text and read the few words at the back of the volume. My sights settled on the final line of text: *"Find Teddy Black at Tattoo Times, 699 LOMBARD STREET, San Francisco, California."*

Reaching for my backpack, I dug my hand down into the pouch to fish out my phone. I snapped a photograph of the page, highlighting the address, and put the book back into its slot on the bottom shelf.

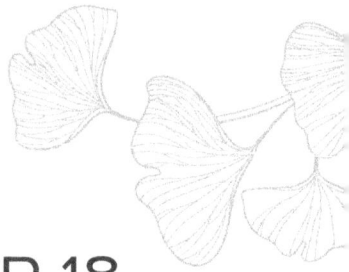

CHAPTER 18

*S*an Francisco was only about thirty miles south from my stop, and the weather gathered strength as I approached. The wind licked at my ankles, forcing me to concentrate fully on the road. Traffic began to slow, and cars surrounded me as my quiet pathway along the coast opened up to access the major city center, the congestion of traffic boxing me in.

Settling into the outside lane, I could see a steep hill at the crest of the next curve and, placed at its peak, gaped the bold, red, steel mouth of the Golden Gate Bridge shrouded in fog. Instantly, I became struck with the memory of watching a documentary with Dylan called *The Bridge* years before. The film had pointed a camera at the mega-structure connecting the city around the clock, capturing twenty-three jumpers falling to their intended deaths. The documentary had been pushed out of my mind until this moment; I had refused to let it find a home in my head or surface.

The jumpers fell to their death in four seconds; not much time to rethink their lives or consider their loved ones. It was 245 feet of freedom, seventy-five miles per hour, then meeting the water of the San Francisco Bay. Dylan watched the documentary intently, not flinching as the men and woman hit the concrete-like surface, and not wincing at the interviews with the family members left behind to reconcile these losses.

I swallowed the saliva gathering in my throat; it felt like a baseball going down. I pictured the rough water's surface littered with bodies, floating, limp, and deconstructed from the impact. How many of them felt regret? How many of them felt nothing at all?

I shifted the bike down and quickly looked over my right shoulder, pulling to the graveled side of the road at the entrance to the bridge. I stared down into the Bay's eye until my gaze stung with the wet, salty air.

"Your bike is making some racket for people trying to sleep, you know," a deep and drawn voice hollered at me, my body jumping with a start.

I looked away from the water over to the shoulder of the road and found myself staring at a disheveled man, his clothing dark, layered, and dingy. He peered at me without another word, studying my motorcycle, my precariously stacked gear strapped to the sissy bar, and staring straight through my glasses, searching for my eyes. I felt naked in front of him, embarrassed that he could tell I was a fraud.

"I'm—I'm sorry," I offered while looking past his dark and thin frame to the side of the embankment, which dropped below the bridge into the heavy fog.

"Well, you should be!" he spat, swinging his arm in the air, gesturing to his home.

"Fucken tourists everywhere! Assholes riding these rented bicycles, motorists honking and taking pictures, and motorbikers like you, Sweetheart, poppin' their pipes not givin' a flying damn about me!" His words were forceful, but not untrue. His shouts traveled clearly over the noise of my bike and through my helmet.

I looked up at the walkway running along the side of the bridge as I idled in traffic, full of visitors crammed in taking photos, huddled in their jackets shielding their bodies from the frigid bursts of air skipping off the ocean. The foggy mist hung in the space around them, stippling their hair with moisture.

"Well, don't just sit there, turn off your bike, woman!" His tone was condescending. I quickly obliged, fumbling for the ignition key.

"Come here," he waved his hand cloaked in a glove, the pointer protruding through the knit casing, motioning to me to follow him.

Rolling my bike to the shoulder, I leaped off the seat, looking anxiously behind me to ensure I kept other tourists within my sightline. Following him, I walked to the edge of the bridge where the hardened clay of the roadside met the end of the pavement and joined the metal surface of the bridge deck. I leaned forward and saw a bucket turned over and a camp stove much like my own with a coffee pot brewing on top.

"I won't bite ya. Come here."

I don't know why, but I followed him the ten steps down the bank and out of sight, out of safety. My heart, pounding.

"Tell me what you're looking for, little mama. What's got you runnin'?" he confronted me instantly. I reached out with the toe of my boot and touched the rim of the overturned bucket.

"Have you ever seen anyone jump off the bridge?" I blurted out, not sure why I opened with this morbid inquiry.

"Well, of course," he retorted, matter of fact, not thrown off by my line of questioning. "There ain't nothin' I haven't seen living under here." He gazed up at the underbelly of the bridge.

"You ever talk to any of the jumpers, you ever save anyone from doing it?" My tone was more aggressive. I took my glasses off and found his eyes as I adjusted to the light.

His brow drew together, creasing in the center. "Well, no." Direct in his reply. "I looked a young girl straight in the face once. She climbed the rail and her leg swung over the side. Middle of the day, too. People everywhere. We locked in, and I think she waited for me to rush over there and grab her coat or something," he paused, wetting his lips. His tongue reached out and sucked in his beard at the corner of his mouth. "I didn't flinch! I gave her a nod and said a prayer that her demons didn't cross over with her. What else you gonna do? There ain't no saving people that don't want saving. Save yourself, shit, that's what I think." He shook his head in an exaggerated manner, disapprovingly. "Well, I know you didn't roll in on that old hog to hang out under the bridge with me. Where you headin'?"

That's the second time I'd been asked where I was going, and for the first time, I thought I had an answer. Digging my phone out of my jacket pocket, I pulled up the snapshot of the address from the book. I tilted the screen over to him and used my hand to block the glare. "Lombard Street, wherever that is," I replied.

"Lombard Street? What you gonna do down there?" he questioned, pulling his body away from me.

"I'm looking for Tattoo Times, Teddy Black's shop," I retorted, faking confidence.

"Teddy Black? What's a girl like you doing looking for old Teddy? You may be here on that bike, but I can tell for miles away you ain't the type of girl to get inked." He scoffed as the words fell from his mouth. "I got me a tattoo from him in '78. Shit, I think that was his first shop even, down on Mission Street when he was a kid." Reaching for his sleeve, he pushed back the worn cloth to reveal a darkened splotch of ink, dusted under the skin from years in the sun. At one time, a rose, the solid bold outlines from a nine-liner still fighting to hold on. "I just waltzed right in that place and picked one straight off the wall," he bragged to me, his chest filling out with pride.

"Well, you're right," I offered. "I don't have any tattoos yet. This will be my first." My plan became clear and real for the first time.

Like staring at a hidden-eye picture for hours, and the shapes began to finally take form. I thought about the drawings wrapped tightly onto the front of the bike, of my bike, and felt anxious to get going. Shuffling between my feet, I pushed my glasses back onto my face.

"I think I need to go. Any advice on how to get there?" I requested, feeling nervous at the thought of navigating traffic.

"You're a brave one; I can feel it," he offered me as a smirk crossed his lips. "There's one rule about San Francisco that you need to know to get anywhere in this city: when you get to the bottom of any hill, you turn right. Wiggle to the right every time, and you'll get there," his mouth spread wide, and I could see the space where his lateral tooth should have been. "Go on now, girl! Get across that bridge." He shooed me with his hand, and I jumped up the bank with a small surge of adrenaline in my system.

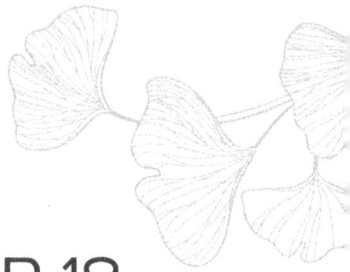

CHAPTER 19

*A*s I arrived at the crest of Lombard Street, shock set in. I'd survived navigating traffic, pedestrians, bicycles, and hill after hill after hill to arrive at my destination. At the top of Lombard Street, I peered down to the bottom to discover it contained eight hairpin turns in a one-block section. The street ran east to west and wove back and forth to minimize the hill's natural 27% grade. My heart thumped in my ears, echoing in my helmet as I took in the descent. The surface of the street sat paved in red brick, and traffic only traveled the road in one direction: down. I waited for maybe 600 feet in length to get to the bottom and arrive at my destination, but I became frozen in fear. The metamorphosis I sought waited at the bottom of these switchbacks, and yet here I sat, petrified, turned to stone, unable to begin the descent.

Do you understand that the world is real, Annalise? I asked myself. The real truths that you must admit to yourself. It was time to stop believing the lie that I would be okay and let the reality of my own life in. The anonymity of being a widow for the last few thousand miles will be behind me at the bottom of this hill, and I'll have to wear the label again.

The widow is the cloak that I cannot shed. It is the lump gathered at the back of my throat, stopping air and life and sustenance and water and sunshine from passing into my system. It sticks to my heels like a shadow, and no matter what direction I turn from the sun, the shape is always cast behind me for others to see.

It tells me that it won't go away; it tells me that I will never be alright. This truth is in my mind, but not on my skin. I have the chance to delete my past and move along, or I can mark my body and carry the dialogue forward every day. This is real; this is all there is. Dylan is real. I felt him push me as my bike inched forward. I slowly released the pressure off the front brake, rolling toward the top of the hill. I pulled back on the throttle, my shadow and Dylan's shadow both clinging tightly to my back.

CHAPTER 20

The front doors of Tattoo Times looked like the entrance to many of the tattoo shops I'd been in before. Hand-painted lettering graced the windows, a neon sign shining proudly in tradition, the word "TATTOO" in bold, capital letters blown out in glass, and light to call the world in.

I pulled back the door and walked inside. The apprehensiveness had dissipated; I'd done this before. The cardboard roll tightly under my arm, and my backpack slung over my shoulder. The familiar smell of CaviCide filled my nostrils and the door sucked closed behind me. The low buzz of coil machines sang out of turn behind the partial wall ahead. A man and a woman sat together on a small sofa in the front entrance, flipping through a portfolio together; they didn't look up when I arrived.

Every inch of the space hung covered in framed tattoo flash, traditionally drawn, inked, and spotted with primary colors. The head of a bulldog baring its teeth and wearing an army helmet, the crossed legs of a nude woman, tipping her sailor's hat at me, a swallow diving off the corner of a page. I looked up, and strung between each side of the hallway dangled a fine rope with cards of flash hanging every few inches. They fluttered like Tibetan prayer flags and turned into shapes as they continued down the hallway, disappearing into the darkness.

I met eyes with a man about my age leaning on the front counter, comfortably wearing a red and black flannel shirt buttoned to the top, and dark-rimmed glasses. He had an unlit cigarette sticking out of the corner of his mouth. Looking at the countertop, I noticed him tracing out a stencil, his pencil resting in place. "Ye-llo," he murmured, the cigarette moving in animation as he formed the syllables.

"Hey," I replied, the word barely escaping my lips.

"You have an appointment or looking for a walk-in?" he questioned. A phrase he likely said a hundred times per day.

"Uh, well, I'm looking for Teddy Black," I gulped. After all this way, I needed to just speak the truth. I stood straight from my spine, engaging my legs and feeling my feet on the floor.

"Teddy? He's retired, you know?" His eyes gestured to a framed black and white photograph of Teddy Black wearing a short-sleeved bowling shirt, arms folded across his chest, showing blurred images wrapping around his forearms.

"I know," I quipped. I had no idea. "I still need to speak to him. How can I get ahold of him?" I pressed, suddenly confident.

He laid his pencil down and held it to the glass countertop with the tip of his finger to not let it roll out of place. He set the other palm flat onto the surface and leaned forward.

"What's it about?" he inquired, still grasping the cigarette with his lips.

I fought a small wave of foolishness that washed up my arms, making its way toward my heart. "I need to talk to him about a kitsune," I pleaded, my fingers reaching to touch the end of the cardboard tube that held the drawings under my arm.

Spotting a shadow near the back of the hallway over his shoulder, I glanced up. A man, half-leaning out from a curtained station at the end of the hall. "Mike!" he hollered, "send her back." The voice carried full and firm.

Blood rushed to my face, and I could feel the heat of his words sweeping over me. Mike nodded and pulled the small, half-saloon door back to let me into the lair. Stepping across the threshold, I walked onto the black and white checkered tiled floor. I turned my face up to the ceiling, watching the flags of flash come in and out of perspective as I neared each row. I reached the final door on the left where I'd seen the figure and turned to fill the doorway.

"What's your name, kid?" he questioned, sitting on a rolling stool leaned over a light table. His hair was grey and curled around his ears, the skin on his bare arms deepened in color by the sun and swirled with fine, white hairs. Blurred tattoos scattered his forearms, causing my eyes to jump from one image to the next like a pinball machine.

"Annalise," I stated, my voice feeling steady and calm.

"Annalise. Annalise. Pretty name." A smile crossed his lips as he turned his neck to seek my glance. "What's this about a kitsune?" he inquired.

Dylan always said tattooers loved to tattoo kitsunes; they had a draw to them that could not be explained.

I searched for my voice. "Well, Mr. Black——"

"Woah, wait a minute!" he chuckled. "Mr. Black? No, just call me Ted." I felt his warmth passing through the air. "Sit," he said as he pulled another wheeled stool from under the desk.

I sat on the stool and faced my knees toward him. "Ted," I smiled, feeling a sudden relaxation take over. I've been here before. I've sat on this stool near this man in this room before. I've looked in on this moment between a tattooer and a customer and felt powerful sitting in this room.

"I have a drawing with me." I pulled the tube to my lap, worked the small plastic cap out of the end, and worked the rolled drawings free. I grasped the corner of the fox and laid it on the desk in front of him, then scrolled the remaining drawings tightly in my hands, sliding them back down the tube. I set the tube aside on the floor, dropping my backpack off next to it.

Teddy smoothed the corners of the drawings, avoiding passing his palms over the pencil lines. He pressed the edges of the filmy paper to release the curl of the tube; he moved his face closer to the lines, his eyes following the curves of each tail of the master fox.

"I don't tattoo other people's drawings, Annalise. I'm sure you know that," he stated without breaking his gaze on the drawing.

"I figured as much," I replied, though I could tell it was not the end of his thought. I waited patiently for him to digest.

"Who drew this?" he inquired, cocking his chin in my direction.

"Dylan," I stated, realizing that wouldn't mean much to him. "My—my husband." My ears began to get hot; I hadn't had this conversation yet, had not rehearsed in my mind.

"He a tattooer?" Teddy turned his knees to me until we were fully square to one another.

"Yes, he is, err, yes. He was." I ran the palms of my hands over the denim on my thighs, creating a numb feeling on the beds of my fingertips.

"I see," Teddy answered. A single, slow nod in my direction showed me he understood.

"A Tattoo Widow," he whispered in a kind tone; he placed his hand on top of mine to steady the anxious movement.

"They leave you for the fame of the needle long before they leave this earth, Annalise," Teddy whispered, shaking his head slowly from side to side, "but you know that."

He understood. I didn't have to hide. He understood. I felt tears building up in my eyes, and I knew I didn't need to hold them back. Silently, I let them roll down my face in relief, my mind filled with the previous decade of dinners alone and attending events by myself. Of Dylan coming and going every few days, of the job sucking him into himself, telling him he was not enough—and of me not understanding. Teddy reached over and swept a tear off my cheek with the back of his calloused knuckle.

"I'm retired, you know?" he said again, waiting for my reaction. I didn't move. I didn't reply.

"You know I'm going to tattoo you though, right?" his voice firm and warm.

Nodding, no words could form, and I felt the consolation and terror and guilt all at once. He turned his body back to the desk and to the drawing. He reached for a roll of tracing paper, pulled free a large swatch, and laid it over Dylan's line. With a red pencil, he lined in a fourth tail onto the shapeshifter and stood back.

"The more tails the kitsune possesses, the wiser he is. You need one more," he affirmed without permission.

I thought back to my journey to get to this shop and agreed silently; another tail seemed fitting. I watched intently as he turned the page to complete the stencil, his hand steady and confident pulling full lines across the paper in single strokes. Having seen this process a hundred or more times, never had I experienced the pressure rising up inside of my body as he neared the completion of the step. Once he finished, he pulled the drawing from the table and held it up between us; the image of his face veiled behind the foggy paper's texture. My gaze shifted focus between him and the fox. Kitsune were typically female, but he kept referring to this static creature as male. He understood.

"Okay?" His voice was light while asking for permission. I nodded, too scared to speak.

I stood from the stool as he turned toward his station to prepare, laying a disposable drop cloth onto the table and pulling rubber gloves over his aged hands. I watched him closely as he stretched a layer of plastic wrap over his side table and smeared a streak of Vaseline onto the tray.

He set two rows of tiny plastic cups onto the jelly and carefully filled each cap with concentrated inks, the colors all appearing dark and thick and dull. He made a second row of black and left a few empty caps at the end of the line.

Observing closely, he selected two machines, one for lining and one for shading. He grabbed the first one without effort and laid it on the table. He began to seek the second machine, slow in his selection. His eyes surveyed the options over and over until he settled on one to the far left that had a cast body made of steel, clearly built by hand and engraved with tiny, crude letters that read "*For Teddy*."

He chose his needles and pulled them free from the sterile plastic sheathing, guiding them into their respective tubes and securing them to the bodies of the machines with small black elastic bands. He carefully pulled barrier bags over the clip cords and the wash bottles; he connected the power supply and held the machine in hand in front of his chest. He pressed his foot onto the pedal and the familiar buzz filled the air. He pulsed the foot pedal a few times and turned the knob slightly on the power supply until he seemed happy with the sound it emitted. He laid the machine gently on its side onto the draped tabletop and pulled a small free-standing lamp closer to the setup. He placed a short plastic cup of water on the side table and a stack of paper towels next to it. He moved through this setup like a habit, quietly letting a whistle escape through his pursed lips.

"Where are we putting him?" he inquired, gesturing to the sly fox awaiting his turn.

"My hip," I replied, touching the soft curve of my leg over my jeans.

"Okay. Let's size it and get started," he noted, assuming me to be familiar with what came next.

I turned and took the jacket off my arms, hanging it on a hook on the wall. Pulling the zipper, I pushed off my boots with the opposite toe. My nervous fingers fumbled to free the button on my pants, shaking as I dropped them to my ankles and stepped out of them to feel the cool air rush to my skin. It prickled with goosebumps as I adjusted to the temperature. I became suddenly aware of the vulnerability of this moment, of the offering of my skin to a man that had touched thousands of visitors before me, seeking a connection through a needle.

Teddy had finished running the drawing through the stencil-making machine and sat piecing together the paper as he turned to look up at me. "Where are the rest of them?" he poked, grinning at my bare legs. "A tattooer's wife without tattoos! This is new," a warm smile filling his face. "It's okay, Annalise. There's a first time for everything." A chuckle escaped his lips, and I blushed in embarrassment.

Floating over to him, I could not feel the ground under my feet. I turned my hip toward his waiting hands as he sat on the stool with his eyes in line with my fleshy, pale skin. He turned the drawing a few degrees in each direction and mumbled, "uh-huh," as he set the stencil back onto the bed. He reached for a bottle of liquid and squirted a small stream onto my hip while I stood next to him, my body retracting from the shock. He rubbed the flattened palm of his hand over my skin until a small film appeared. He reached for a blue razor and flicked the plastic cover off the blade. Feeling my skin tighten, he pulled the razor down in long fluid strokes towards my knee, shaving off the fine blonde hairs on my thigh. He reached for a second bottle and washed the leg clean. Glancing down, I saw my flesh slightly raised and warm.

He applied a thick, white gel from a small squeeze bottle onto my thigh and spread it evenly over the fresh skin using the side of his pinky. Then, he reached for the stencil and hovered it over my hip as he cocked his head to view it.

Once pleased with the position, he pressed his finger into the center of the stencil until it clung to the gel on my leg; he then smoothed the stencil from the center out to the edges of the paper.

My skin felt the tickle of his gloved hands as they followed the curve of my body, wrapped down my thigh, and around the shape of my buttock. I could see the shapeshifter's image seeping through the stencil paper, blurred purple lines forcing themselves to the surface. Watching closely, he peeled the stencil paper back from the top right corner, carefully revealing each tail whipping in circles around my flesh. I felt the power of the fox begin to take hold, and I looked down into his eyes and outstretched front legs.

"Take a look," Teddy offered, gesturing at the mirror on the wall.

Stepping in front of my reflection, avoiding my face, I stared down into the eyes of the kitsune. I followed the lines of each powerful tail and stopped to examine the new tail Teddy had added to the drawing. I nodded.

"I'll take that as a yes," he offered, patting his hand on the draped table. "Lie down, face away from me here so I can get to work," he directed. His routine began to take hold.

Climbing onto the firm padded bed, I felt self-conscious as my bare skin was being presented before him. I laid on my side, watching the kitsune stretch out of shape, and my flesh tightened across my outstretched limb. Feeling my stomach fall to the side, I clenched my muscles, holding in nerves. Sweat began to collect on my lip, and my hands felt sticky as I laid them folded under the side of my face, hearing the paper draping crinkle with each tensed movement.

"Annalise," I heard Teddy's voice from over my shoulder, holding very still as he spoke. "I'll take care of you, just breathe in real deep. He knows you're here; he wants you to be here," he offered, pressing his hand over my thigh, welcoming the kitsune to the room.

I blew my breath out in a small, steady stream, releasing the tension in my stomach and letting the flesh of my belly relax in place.

Feeling a cool swipe of his finger, he smeared a line of petroleum jelly over the tip of a tail; I knew what this meant. He was going to begin. The machine whined as he pressed power into it through his foot, tapping it to check the currency out of habit. The buzz of the machine moved closer to me as I felt his fingers press hard into my skin, stretching the surface tight with his free hand.

The frequency of the machine's murmur deepened and became a droning sound as the liner hit my leg, burying beneath the skin and changing into a long, slow foghorn sound. My feet clenched at the first feeling of the pain, a shallow and steady sting crossing my skin and shooting down my leg. I tensed, holding my fingers tightly together, waiting for relief. Relief did not come though, the warmth spread further over my body, and slowly I relaxed and allowed it to hum in my limbs.

My body absorbed the vibration from the machine, accepting each tiny pulse of the needle's tip as it entered and exited my dermis. I could feel the kitsune growing, its shape gathering life, and its spirit forming within me.

The needle's drag pulled at my fibers, causing sharp pains to enter in one location on my thigh and exit at a remote location down in my foot and calf.

The process consumed me as my nervous system fought off the hands of Teddy and Dylan at once. I could feel Dylan's shadow clinging to the end of the bed, coaxing me to continue and telling me to give up at the same time. Turning my face, the bright lamp glared at me and let the light hit my eyelids. I saw red through the thin skin and felt the warmth of the bulb on my cheeks. I relaxed my toes, unclenching them in a wave and allowing my hands to go limp. I felt heat radiating from my hip as the kitsune gained life and seeped under my skin.

"The kitsune is Japanese, you know?" Teddy offered me, not looking up or breaking the rhythm of the machine's pace in his hand. I did not reply; he knew I was aware. "I studied in Japan, '73. Good times over there. Sailor Jerry finished up with me and sent me overseas to get highly-evolved or something." He smirked, a chuckle in his voice at his own comment. "See, the Japanese and the Americans were tattooing in two different worlds in the '70s, not seeing each other's stuff except for in the occasional book, or if you were lucky, on a man that would stop by Jerry's shop and show it off. I was with the master, Horihide." He shook his head slowly, bringing the memory to life.

I laid still, my ears reaching for the next thought.

"Horihide, a God, an absolute master. I'd never seen anything like that back here in California; I'd been on this coast my whole life. I knew traditional American, and he showed me the East." He paused, and I could hear him lick his lips.

I didn't want him to stop. Holding as still as possible, I waited.

"He had a mandala on his back, that's a Buddhist prayer symbol, and it was surrounded by a dragon. Powerful man, Horihide. Beautiful man." Lost in his own mind, back in Japan on the floor of Horihide's studio, crouched over a willing man offering his body. "I came home, and I never drew the same again. Everything I made after that day I returned, it's part American and part Japanese. Even if I don't want it to be, I can't stop it." His hand paused, and I felt a cool relief as he sprayed my leg with a cleansing liquid and wiped away the ink and blood momentarily. The rough surface of the paper towel dragged over the fresh wound, but strangely brought a moment of freedom.

"You know, he taught me about the kitsune. He told me the tale of the nasty fox, and how it would shapeshift, and get in trouble. Don't ever cross the fox."

I waited, my leg numb from the constant needle, my body alive.

"Lots of lore about the old fox. He told me an ancient story about a servant that had headed home at sundown in Kai, and he spotted a fox. He chased down the fox with a noisemaker that you'd use to scare off a dog, maybe. He shot at the fox and hit 'em right in the back leg!"

Excitement climbed in his voice as if he were there.

"The fox cried out and limped into the bushes and out of sight. The servant went after his arrow, and the fox jumped right out in front of him, that bastard!"

He told me the tale as if it had just happened to him the other day. Animation filled his low, steady voice, but didn't interrupt his hands. I could feel he'd switched from the liner and was onto the shading machine, pushing color into my skin. He was making small, slow circles with the machine, a much duller sensation. He paused every few minutes to refill the needle with ink, to wash the excess blood away, and to apply more Vaseline.

"He was about to shoot this fox again, and bam, the fox just disappears!" his pitch heightened for the slightest moment to punctuate his tale. "He spotted the fox up the road, running ahead while spurring his horse along; the fox carried a flaming brand in his mouth. The fox reached the servant's house and when he got close, he turned into a human. He set the servant's house on fire without a single hesitation." There wasn't a trace of disbelief in his retelling of the folklore; he'd heard it many times before. "The servant tried to shoot the transformed man when he got close, but he turned back into a fox and ran away."

His tone became matter-of-fact as the story had come to its climax. "The house burned straight to the ground. Swift vengeance, the old kitsune; it's best to leave them alone." And with that, the story was over, and his point was made. It was best to leave them alone.

My joints ached, and my limbs were filled with shooting pains as I laid twisted across the narrow bed, frozen in the moment. I'd been holding the position for hours, despite the few short breaks I'd been granted. My nervous system fought back through a tiny shake taking over my body. Teddy had risen and moved my body in place over the course of the hours that passed; he worked around me like a sundial, marking the minutes that we'd gathered together in this moment. My arms and legs ached and stiffened as his shadow lazily cast over the floor behind him.

The tattoo progressed down my leg further and further until he neared my knee. I knew it was coming close to being finished, and I was scared for it to be over. I didn't want to be left alone with the kitsune and be responsible for the shapeshifter, already taking a hold of me, changing my physical form. Bringing my hands in front of my face, I examined my fingers. I pictured them growing long and thin and lanky; they wrapped around my torso and encased my body like the roots of an old tree. The fingertips laced into one another and the kitsune clung tightly around my ribs, making it hard to breathe. Relaxing into the sensation, I felt calm and shrouded with safety; the fox secured its tails around me and provided warmth. Picturing my rooted fingers releasing their grasp, I felt Teddy rubbing my hip with his hand, the machine silent.

"Okay, Annalise. Please, hop up." Over, just like that.

Pushing myself up onto my elbow, I allowed the blood to circulate through my arms and neck. I straightened my leg and flexed my foot, extending and bending at the knee a few times. I still didn't look down. Swinging my legs over the side of the table, I sat up properly with my hands planted firmly at either side.

My feet touched the ground feeling unsteady, and I scooted forward as the paper drape stuck to my thigh with blood and ink and fluids. I pulled the cloth free of my skin and walked cautiously toward the mirror on the wall with my eyes focused on my stockinged feet. Inching closer to the mirror, I watched my shadow casting onto the floor; I could see Dylan's shape in the black silhouette behind me waiting patiently. Turning my hip toward my reflection, I looked up, finding Teddy's eyes in the mirror.

He'd lived this moment thousands of times before, the anticipation of the reveal. The judgment of the permanent adornment he'd stroked on the skin. My abdomen tightened as my eyes fell to meet the kitsune. The bold stride glided down my leg, sweeping over my hip, and the tails wrapped around me in a powerful embrace. Solace washed through my veins as the essence of his form moved on my skin. I examined the small stipples of blood speckling the surface of my shining skin, patterning the fox's golden coat, the body flexing in motion as I moved my muscles.

"Do good with it," Teddy stated matter-of-factly, nodding at the shapeshifter. He understood the power of the transformative creature. "Don't let him turn you into something you're not." He turned his back to me and began cleaning up his station, methodically giving me a moment alone in the looking glass.

The kitsune rearranged my physiological features, manipulating my anatomy. It forced me to stand straight and mimicked Dylan's confidence. He surged through me, multiplying my soul and making room for both of us to exist inside of me, filling in the tiny gaps Dylan had left. The empty spaces closed slightly, letting in less light and starving out the hurt. My hands felt warm and slackened, and my voice felt strong and confident.

"I will still be me," I promised Teddy, my voice deepened and brawny. I saw him nod deeply in the reflection over my shoulder as I watched the kitsune, his tails pointing to the door.

CHAPTER 21

Heading east, the Shovelhead rattled underneath me. The heat of the sun bore through my pants and stung on my freshly tattooed hip. The rough texture of the denim pressed into the creases of my thigh and my skin felt hot and tender. I placed my palm firmly onto the kitsune to dampen the vibration of the bike running through my leg and leaned into the throttle until the wind took hold and pushed me forward. Riding on the I-80, I climbed out of California and crossed over the Nevada border. The night before fell cold, and I'd gotten up early to ride into the sun, seeing my breath in the morning air. A bandana secured tightly over my nose and lip, I tilted my chin into my body to stay warm and shield my face from the wind.

With the sun beating directly onto my face, I could smell a distinct filth fill my nostrils. Grey-blue smoke began to rise from between my knees and blur my line of vision as the bike lurched beneath me. Panic filled my hands as I shifted down and veered off to the shoulder of the narrow road. I pulled onto the uneven gravel and drug my feet to a stop in the packed dirt, fear filling my chest. Smoke billowed from every crevice of the bike, encasing my arm as I reached out to turn the ignition off. Hopping off the bike, I stepped back a few feet, crouching down and balancing myself with my hands. Tears were welling up in my eyes; Dylan was trying to stop me from going on. I clawed at the dirt beneath me and threw a handful of dusty clay and pebbles at the smoldering bike.

"No!" I screamed into the bandana covering my mouth and nose. I pulled it down around my neck as I gasped for breath between heaving cries.

"No, Dylan. No. Just let me go!" I wailed, demanding freedom as the smoke found me and gathered around me like a cocoon.

"What am I doing here?" I whispered to myself, dirt sticking to the tears streaking my face.

Who was I kidding? I thought. I pushed off my toes and tipped back onto the dirt, running my hand over the kitsune under my jeans, feeling embarrassed. Pulling my helmet from my head, I rubbed a gloved hand over my matted hair, smoke stinging my eyes and burnt metal filling my nostrils. Spit stuck to my chin as I coughed without raising my hand. I tilted my head back until my neck strained, squeezing my eyes shut as tightly as I could, willing myself back home into my childhood bedroom, my mother sitting at the side of my bed with my back turned to her.

I heard a vehicle approaching and I hung my head, turning my face away from the road. Ashamed of my position, I willed them to pass by me and let me continue on in my pity. I could hear the familiar sound of a standard transmission shifting down, coming to a stop, the tires grabbing at the gravel shoulder near me. I looked up and saw an emerald green single-cab Ford pickup truck with extended chrome mirrors protruding from the sides. It had rust creeping in on the left side of the grill and was missing the *F* in "FORD" so it read *O R D* in widely spaced capital letters.

The truck came to a stop; I heard the engine turn to rest and the heavy hinged doors open. I could see both occupants were wearing cowboy boots, crepe-soled and worn deep into the creases. Real cowboy boots. My eyes followed up their legs, denim-clad and well fitted.

"Sled giving you trouble there?" a deep and gravelly voice offered. I met his eyes, in his late sixties, hands on his hips. A worn button-down plaid shirt tucked neatly into his jeans with a native-patterned leather belt cinched around his waist.

"Guess so," I said with apathy. Defeat.

My eyes shifted to the other figure, a woman of the same age. Her hair placed in a long silver braid that fell over her shoulder, strands sticking out down the length of the braid and catching the light behind them. She took purposeful strides toward me and got into a crouch. She put her worn hand on my shoulder, a ring on every finger of silver and turquoise.

"Get up," Her voice was gruff but gentle. I could tell she had kids my age. I obliged, shifting onto one knee and pushing my weight up with my hand on my thigh.

"Phil," said the man, extending his hand. I shook it, and his sturdy fingers encased mine.

"Donnalu," the woman chimed in, nodding her chin deeply towards me.

"Annalise," I stated, suddenly feeling silly for crying.

"Grab your lid. We'll load ya up." Phil's voice sounded like he'd chain-smoked unfiltered cigarettes since child-hood. I reached for my helmet and walked over to the bike.

"Shovelheads are fussy, but always worth the trouble," he affirmed.

"So I've heard," I smirked, shaking my head.

Phil grabbed her by the bars and released the kickstand. He pushed her over to the rear of his truck and gestured for us to come help.

"Where you off to?" Donnalu questioned.

"Reno." My voice relaxed.

Phil had steadied the bike with one hand and released the tailgate with the other. He backed the truck over to the edge of the road where the bank sloped down, creating an easy ramp and leveling the ground. I could see a wide wood plank laying the length of the bed of the truck.

"Grab that for me, Annalise" he gestured at the board.

I put one knee up on the corrugated tailgate and reached into the truck to grab the wood. I made a ramp between the truck, the bank, and the road as Phil circled the bike over to load it up. The angle wasn't steep; he had done this before. He rocked the front tire of the bike onto the wide ramp and began to walk the bike towards the truck. I balanced behind the bike and grabbed onto the rear fender, pushing from behind and steadying it up the ramp. It lurched over the crease in the tailgate, and into the bed as I steadied it into place. I held it straight as Phil hopped into the bed and rummaged for red tie-downs that had faded to pink in the sun. He worked methodically and cinched the bike down tight into the bed, giving the bars a firm shake to make sure his handiwork was sufficient. Once satisfied with the job, we hopped down and he propped the board back into the bed, wedging it against the tie-down along the side.

"Jump in the cage, gals," as he gestured to the cab.

Donnalu climbed into the middle seat, and I crawled in next to her. The vinyl dashboard had a large crack riddled across it; a thin layer of dust settled into the fine-textured surface. The bench seat had piping along the edge of the dirt-filled upholstery, creased with the weight of Donnalu's body riding shotgun for many miles. I rolled the window down a few inches and fastened the seatbelt across my lap. Donnalu placed her hand onto Phil's leg and let it rest in place, probably out of habit.

"Reno, hey?" Phil confirmed.

"Yeah, that's my plan," I chuckled.

"I know where you can get fixed up. Don't worry about it." He looked past his wife and gave me a toothy smile, the edges of his teeth a deep yellow.

I could smell the smoke from my bike in my sleeves, but I became relaxed.

"Okay, Phil," I agreed. "Let's go, then." I didn't know where we were heading, but that was fine.

I rubbed my hand over the kitsune and summoned him to lead me.

They talked amongst themselves for a few miles, and I watched out the window at the scenery changing from greens to reds. They were comfortable with a stranger in their small and private space, making me feel safe.

Looking at Phil's visor, I noticed an old black and white photograph pinned there. It featured a young man riding a wild mustang, arm outstretched in the air and dirt flying from the hooves of the powerful animal blurred in the background.

"Is that you?" I questioned, my eyes trained on the picture.

"Well, it *was* me, darling." He smiled. A deep cough escaped his throat as the corners of his eyes creased at the memory. "I hitchhiked this road right about your age," he told me, looking out the windshield onto the road ahead.

He had one elbow bent and resting on the window frame, and the other hand held the bottom of the wheel with two large fingers looped around it. The road proved straight and narrow.

"I walked for nearly a day before I got picked up. Just out the service and making my way home."

I tried to imagine him in uniform, remembering the comfortable but tidy dressing of his clothing today when I first surveyed him.

"An old fella eventually stopped for me in his pickup truck about dusk, and when I got into the cab, a pistol on the seat." He rubbed his nose with the back of his hand. "I was scared shitless! But I was tired and hungry. He told me to shoot at the road signs to help him stay awake. After three years in the service, I'd handled a few firearms so I grabbed that old pistol and rolled down the window and steadied my hands on the frame."

He took his arm off the window and raised it in front of his face forming a pistol with his fingers. He pulled the trigger, closing one eye, "bang, bang." He chuckled. "I shot at every damn sign on the I-80 across the Nevada desert! I don't think I hit a damn thing; my sphincter clenched up the whole time!"

Donnalu swatted at him playfully, smirking. I glanced back up at the picture on the visor and imagined Phil as a young man, with smoothed skin and a muscular build. Silence fell over the cab and I let them take me wherever it was we were going.

I looked at my bike in the side mirror, watching it vibrate in the bed of the truck as if being ridden by a ghost.

CHAPTER 22

*W*hen I awoke, my neck felt stiff and was throbbing, and my hands were asleep. I felt a pothole jump beneath the truck; it jolted me back to the reality of the bench seat, and that I was sitting three-across in a stranger's pickup. The kitsune itched on my leg and the skin began to dry out as the lines were settling and forming a layer of peeling dried flakes in various colors that clung to the inside of my jeans.

"Look who's back from the dead," Donnalu grinned gently, patting my leg tenderly.

"Just in time. We're here," she said, wherever here happened to be.

I looked ahead as we turned down a quiet alleyway and pulled up to the garage door with a crudely painted *NO PARKING* scrolled across the creased metal in worn white paint. My mind registered back to the small piece of graffiti outside of Dylan's shop scribed on the brick.

Two Harleys were parked at the back door, both well-seasoned. Even stripped of their emblems I could recognize them, the front forks both leaning to the left while resting on their respective kickstands.

"Are we in Reno?" I questioned, having imagined it would look more like a smaller version of Las Vegas rather than an old Western.

"Close enough," nodded Phil, his voice warm and kind.

He pulled the truck to a stop next to the bikes, the gravel beneath the tires crunching under us. "Wait here, gals," Phil instructed as he stepped out of the cab, leaving the door ajar behind him.

He disappeared into the main door to the side. I could feel my throat tighten, overwhelmed. *How did I end up here, in a stranger's truck in the middle of nowhere with Dylan's broken-down bike?* I thought. He'd be furious with me; I wanted to feel his anger, his disdain. I wanted to feel the heat of his words as they landed on my face, my body filled with fear worrying about his next move.

Clenching my jaw, I contorted my mouth into an awkwardly shaped crescent to hold in the tears. Donnalu looked straight forward, still seated tightly next to me. She grabbed my hand and gave it a light squeeze.

"This is all part of it," she offered. I blew a slow and steady stream of air out from between my shaking lips and sucked in a breath through my nostrils.

"My husband hung himself," I blurted out.

I stared through the windshield, letting my eyes fix on the exploded yellow streaks of bugs gathered from the highway. I had not said it out loud before, and I felt ashamed.

"I didn't know," I whispered, not sure of what I had confessed to. I didn't know. "I guess you could say I'm running away," I grinned.

"Where are you going?" Donnalu questioned, still holding my hand.

"I have no idea, Donnalu," I replied. "You know how they say that when you die, you go into purgatory? I'm Italian; my family believes in that shit. Anyway, it's this place, this in-between layer after you physically die. They make you wait there before you can go to heaven so they can purify you first, or something." I shifted the weight between my hips. "They lay out all of your sins, and God comes and looks at them. They try to change your soul by praying over you and judging you. They look at you and go, 'oh yeah, she indulged here, she fucked up there,' and all this crazy shit."

I remembered reading every word about purgatory in Catechism class at seven or eight years old, obsessing with this idea of dying and then picturing being stuck floating while everyone looked back at all of the horrible ways you hurt people in your life, as if watching at a drive-in movie.

"They are trying to purify you or something," I shrugged. "It's like you can get stuck there forever, I think. I don't know if it's everlasting or just temporary or what. It's like this layer between when you die and when you rest in heaven, or they send you down to hell to burn. That's where I'm stuck. Dylan, he's in hell. He didn't wait in purgatory; he went straight to the fiery gates and knocked," I chuckled. "The real joke is that he's gone, and I'm the one trapped in this layer of divine judgment, but I'm still alive." I didn't know why I tried to explain this feeling, but I continued to ramble.

"It's this place where everyone is trying to cleanse me of Dylan's sin, where everyone is whispering about me, asking how I could have let this happen. It's seriously so fucked up. It's like I'm stuck in the church's confessional on my knees, and no matter how many Hail Mary's they tell me to repeat in repentance, they will not let me leave limbo." I was certain I wasn't making any sense at this point, but it felt like such a relief to identify it.

"So, I had to run away." It suddenly seemed a lot more obvious to me.

"Can I tell you a quick story?" Donnalu spoke after a long pause. She seemed nervous by my rant.

"Of course," I turned to face her, examining the organically shaped sunspots on her lined cheek. They looked like amoebas under a microscope lens.

"Well, I want to tell you how I know God isn't even real," she turned, scooting her body to the driver's seat and resting her knee on the bench between us so she could face me square-on.

"I have a daughter, right about your age. When she was a little girl, I sent her to Sunday school because, well, that's what everyone did." She smiled, her words slow and soft. "After church service, she came out from Sunday school and found me out on the grass in front of the parish where I stood with the other Moms, gossiping, I'm sure. She had a paper in her hand, and I asked if I could see it." She chuckled at the memory. "I looked at the paper and asked her, 'What is it?' I saw across the top of the photocopied sheet it said *DRAW A PICTURE OF WHAT GOD LOOKS LIKE.* I looked at the paper, and I looked at her—I didn't see a bearded man in a long, draped cloak. I was confused."

She pulled a small strand of hair from the corner of her mouth, and continued.

"It looked like a bird to me, a bird in a hat or something! So, I asked her, you know, 'Honey, what do you think God looks like?' and she said to me, 'Mama, you know the lollipop suckers? You know the owl that says, 'How many licks does it take to get to the center?' Well, that's God.' Stunned. She had drawn an owl wearing a graduation cap, just like in the commercials!" A big smile took over Donnalu's face, shaking her head softly in memory. "About the most accurate thing I'd ever heard! My kid thought God was a talking owl wearing a graduation cap, sucking on a lollipop! Well, we never went back to church again!"

Laughing at Donnalu, I pictured the paper, and realized she was right.

"People say you have this 'Come to Jesus' moment in your life, right? Well, I had quite the opposite. Jesus is a bird and my daughter helped me see it!"

We both began to giggle. I felt good. I felt safe.

"So, as I see it, you're not running away. You're just seeing how many licks it takes to get to the center of the lollipop." A single nod punctuated her story.

"Okay, girls!" I heard Phil call from outside the driver's door. He pulled it open and leaned his head in. "Let's unload,"

With that, we crawled across the cab and exited the door as he held it for us.

CHAPTER 23

"*N*onna?!" I hollered out, wandering between rooms in her small house. "Nonna!"

No reply.

Her bedroom door was closed tightly; it was never closed. I stepped lightly on my toes toward the door and turned the knob as quietly as I could. Pressing my face to the crack in the door, I let my eyes adjust to the light. I could see her sitting on the end of her bed, her knees covered in her dark brown house dress and a small lace cloth placed over the crown of her head. In her hands, she clutched her rosary and a worn piece of paper.

"Nonna?" I whispered, scared to interrupt her prayer.

"Bella," she replied, waving for me to come in and join her.

I pushed myself up onto the end of the bed next to her and scooted back until I balanced in place.

"What's that?" I asked, pointing at the picture I could see in her grasp.

I curled my feet under me, my shoes tucked against the bed.

"Annalise! Take-a your shoes off the bed!" Nonna cried out. "*Sfortuna,* very bad luck." Her voice was calming as I swung my legs free in front of me.

She looked down, turning the worn card to face me. I saw a painting of a man crudely drawn, covered in a brown cloak with his hand open and in offering.

"This is-a Saint Francis of Assisi," she replied, tapping the picture with her crooked finger.

"He-a my protector," she explained, passing me the card to hold.

The corners were worn smooth, and the paper felt soft in my fingers.

"When I was-a born, my-a Momma name me Francis for-a him. I-a born on-a October four." Her fingers pinched together, gesturing through her story.

"This-a day is a day for Francis, it is the day for-a his Feast."

I nodded slowly at her tale, thinking it strange that her parents named her after a man. "He is a patron for-a the animali," she gestured her hands as if she were herding dogs at our feet. "He-a take care of all of the animali, and his-a heart very, very big. I-a say a his-a prayer every day. He-a care for the poor people, and he love the nature. You-a practice," she instructed, pointing at the card.

I turned the card over and found his prayer scribed in plain text.

Lord, make me an instrument of your peace:
where there is hatred, let me sow love;
where there is injury, pardon;
where there is doubt, faith;
where there is despair, hope;
where there is darkness, light;
where there is sadness, joy.

O divine Master, grant that I may not so
much seek
to be consoled as to console,
to be understood as to understand,
to be loved as to love.
For it is in giving that we receive,
it is in pardoning that we are pardoned,
and it is in dying that we are born to
eternal life.
Amen.

She reached over and pulled the card gently from my grasp when I finished, and flattened it between her palms, rosary strung between her fingers. She resumed her prayer and I waited, patiently, for her to finish in silence.

CHAPTER 24

*S*tanding in the garage, I felt anxious as my bike got assessed. Phil introduced me to Daniel, the shop's proprietor. He was a couple of years older than me, his hair long and tucked behind his ears. He wore faded navy blue coveralls, the sleeves tied around his waist like a belt, revealing a stained and aged t-shirt from a softball tournament in '98. He had a worn tattoo of a seagull that sat between his thumb and pointer finger on the back of his right hand; the wings flexed when he reached out to shake my hand. I felt his callouses roughly grace my palm as his fingers firmly wrapped around mine. His teeth were surprisingly white, flickering through his smile. I watched a few other men in darkly colored coveralls crouching at their stations, struck by how quiet it was in this space.

Phil and Donnalu had loaded back into their truck and were heading out. Donnalu gave me a tight, long hug before she left that clung to my limbs.

She stroked my back and said to me, "The owl is in charge, Annalise. The rest isn't real."

I watched them drive off, knowing that I'd never see them again.

I stood back from Daniel and one of the colleagues that came to help him; they knelt around the Shovelhead and examined the engine, speaking to one another in low voices, the occasional laugh escaping the huddle. I watched them kneeling and tilting their faces, examining various parts on the bike, feeling sheepish that I couldn't even explain what had happened.

"I put oil in every time I filled up with gas!" I shouted out of nowhere.

Daniel looked over his shoulder. I could see him smiling. "Annalise, don't you worry, this is definitely not your fault," he offered, easing my mind. "Shovels always had problems with running hot," he told me matter-of-factly. This had become a theme.

"Classic case here. The oil just pooled in the crankcase rather than getting pumped through. It gets hotter than a firecracker, and there you have it, smokin' on the side of the road in the Nevada desert, waiting for a rescue." He smirked and gave me a wink. "You're just lucky the valves didn't stick and destroy the top end of this girl. We'll make a coupla mods and have you back on the road in no time."

Smiling back, I felt a bit more settled.

"I see this all the time," he continued on, turning back to the bike. "Guys come in here, trying to stop the oil leak with a gasket, but the gaskets can't take the heat."

I could see him tugging at part of the engine, kneeling on one knee.

"You have to get in there with sealant, that's the only way to go."

I nodded, though no one noticed.

He stood up and turned to me, taking a few large strides, soon standing within a couple of feet. He wove a rag in his fingers, reminding me of my Nonna's rosary.

"Annalise, we will fix you up. This bike won't let you down; they never do. It's going to take us a few hours, so you're gonna be stuck here for the night," he told me, waving his hand over his head to let me know that this was now my fortress.

"Why don't you head upstairs? We're gonna be a while, here. I live up there. It's nothing much, but there's a shower and a bed and a little kitchenette. Why don't you go get cleaned up and have a rest? I'll come find ya when I'm done. I'll take the couch tonight; you go ahead and get settled in." Grateful, but unsure, I began to move across the floor. *Why were these strangers so willing to help me?* I thought. *Shouldn't I just get a hotel?* I thought. *How far of a walk would that be?*

I peered up to the second floor, seeing fogged windows and a yellow bulb glowing behind the private glass.

"Oh, o-kay," I hesitated, not expecting these instructions, but accepting the offer.

Bending down, I retrieved my backpack and the tube of drawings. As I turned, he reached out and touched my forearm.

"Help yourself to whatever it is you might need up there, seriously."

I smiled and climbed up the stairs without another word.

Upstairs appeared dimly lit and well-lived-in, a futon in the corner, facing a record player with two bookshelves on either side. The shelves were stacked carelessly, filled with hardcovers, paperbacks, and coil-bound manuals. I walked to the bookshelves and stopped at the futon first. Sitting on the edge, I shrugged off my backpack and unlaced my boots. Flexing my toes, I scrunched them onto the area rug placed underneath the coffee table, two milk crates topped with a piece of painted plywood.

I weaved my way between the table and the couch over to the shelf on the left and began to examine the titles haphazardly displayed on the shelves. Many were art books, mixed together with sections of fiction, surprisingly sorted by author. There were six titles by Tom Robbins in the top left corner, followed by three Kurt Vonnegut's. A smile found my mouth, surprised by Daniel's tastes in reading. There were manuals for Hondas, Harleys, and Suzukis mixed throughout the shelves, representing various years and models, dirtied and folded post-it notes cascading like waves down each edition.

My eyes stopped halfway through the third shelf. Pushed to the back, I could see a familiar title jumping out at me: *Zen and the Art of Motorcycle Maintenance.* I reached for it instinctually, pulling it free and running my hand over the embossed paperback cover.

I opened the first page and saw a handwritten note, *"Danny Boy, get your shit together. Love, Q."*

My eyes retraced that sentence a few times before I flipped the book over and fanned the pages to scan through. There were notes, highlights, and underlines throughout. This book had been read and understood and absorbed and followed. Finding one page dog-eared in the bottom right corner, and I stopped there to read.

Highlighted, circled, and underlined, a simple line of text worshiped in this novel. It read, *"The pencil is mightier than the pen."* I ran my finger over this line and tried to suck its power off of the page. I stepped back over to the sofa and sat with my feet tucked under me.

I read it again. And again. *And again. Erase it. Go back. Change it. It's not permanent,* I thought. I closed the book over my finger, pressing my grip onto the sentence but hiding the page from sight. Leaning my head back, I felt the stretch in the front of my neck, swallowing deeply over and over, listening to the ribbit sound it produced in my ears. I placed the novel next to where I sat, open to this page, faced down on the cushion.

Wandering the rest of the apartment, I found the bathroom: a pedestal sink, toilet, shower in the corner, mirror, and a clawfoot tub. I walked to the tub and turned on the water, rinsing out the basin. Reaching for the plug, I secured it in place, listening to the water hit the coated cast-iron with force as it filled.

I pulled my clothes off, discarded them onto the floor, and placed a towel on the edge of the tub. I stopped the water and stepped my feet in as I sat on the edge, being careful to keep the healing kitsune dry. Leaning forward, I watch my breasts fall shapeless, and my stomach roll over itself. I ran water up my arms, and goosebumps took over my skin. I splashed the water on my face and under my arms. I stood and turned to dunk my hair under the water, scrubbing my scalp with my nails. Twisting my wet hair into a cord down my shoulder, I moved it carefully to the side to stop it from dripping on my leg. I stared down at the fox and looked at the tip of each tail curling on my flesh. I stretched out my leg and flicked the plug free with my toe, concentrating on the tiny whirlpool of water being sucked away.

Standing, I wrapped the towel around my body and went to grab my backpack for fresh clothes.

I dug into the bottom of my bag, towel fitted tightly around me and tucked under my arm. I felt for the small tube of Polysporin and pulled it free. Squeezing a pea-sized amount onto my thigh, I rubbed it over the kitsune, watching it come alive with a high-gloss coating. The skin nearly fully renewed and Teddy's work settled in. I was used to seeing the sleek shape on my leg now, no longer surprised by its existence. I dressed in my remaining clean outfit and smoothed the wrinkles on the front of my t-shirt, though it didn't help.

In the kitchen, there were small, open shelves over a single-basin sink. Lining the shelves were an assortment of mismatched glasses and mugs. I reached for the nearest mug and rinsed it under the tap, swirling the water in the vessel and pouring it down the drain. A bottle of red wine sat pushed to the back corner of the counter, a third-down; I pulled the cork and stuck the bottle under my nose, taking in a deep whiff. It smelled fresh, and I poured it generously into the mug. Setting the mug and the rest of the bottle on the plywood tabletop, I bent down in front of the record player.

I ran my fingers through the stacks of records, not knowing what to expect. The smell of the cardboard sleeves floated up into the space. Landing on Tom Waits, *The Heart of Saturday Night*, I pulled the record carefully from the cover and then from the sleeve inside, holding it up to my face and blowing on each side. Setting it onto the turntable,

I placed the needle down on the eighth track, "Please Call Me, Baby." Making my way back to the futon, I propped myself into the corner, wedging a pillow behind me to recline while keeping my mug of wine afloat.

I retrieved Daniel's copy of *Zen and the Art of Motorcycle Maintenance*, even though my own copy hid in my backpack. I picked up where I'd left off, *"The pencil is mightier than the pen,"* I read again.

Nestled on the couch for a long while, I heard heavy footsteps climbing the perforated metal tread on the stairs. My body tightened up, realizing I'd made myself at home, and fearing the awkwardness that awaited Daniel's arrival. His silhouette filled the fogged window-pane in the door as he turned the lever handle.

"Well, good news," he grinned, his beard casting shadow-like snakes onto his chest from the overhead bulb. "She's running good as new!" A smile filled his face.

"Thanks, Daniel," I replied as genuine relief washed over me.

"I need to get cleaned up," he gestured, heading to the bathroom.

I stayed still on the couch, listening to the muffled sounds of him undressing, and the water running in the room next door with no insulation between us.

"I love this album," I heard him shouting from the bathroom, hearing his deep baritone voice singing along to the track.

He returned, dressed in fresh clothing, his wet hair combed straight and tucked tightly behind his ears, a smooth center part. He had a beer in his hand and he plopped down on the sofa next to me. I tensed.

"You found my favorite book," he grinned, pointing to the paperback spread in my lap.

"I thought it was *my* favorite book," I retorted, "until I opened your copy and realized my level of understanding pales in comparison!" I flipped through the pages, showing off the notes in the margins.

"Yeah, well," he rubbed his shoulder with his free hand, an involuntary action to relieve the pain of his work. "My ex took off on me, and all she left me was this book," He shifted in his seat. "I guess you take it as a sign or whatever. Once in a while, you pay attention." He shook his head lightly to rattle the memory out.

"I hear that," I replied, leaning my mug into his beer bottle, lightly touching them together in a cheers.

"So, what are you doing out this way, anyway?" he asked. Instantly comfortable with a stranger in his home.

"I'm heading into Reno," I responded, offering no further details.

"Reno, hey? You a gambler? A better? Working off a debt? Don't tell me you're a dancer, I'd never buy it!" he teased, a deep chuckle escaped his throat.

I laughed in return, feeling light from the wine. "Nah, none of the above." I sat, staring at his hand clutched around the bottle.

"I'm actually heading that way for a tattoo." It came out easier this time; I'd done this before.

There was a tattooer in Reno that Dylan had never met, but he always obsessed over her work. She tattooed in bold black lines, minimal shading, and no color. Her work looked like an ornate pattern on an Eastern gift, wrapped and presented with a bow, but it had a darkness to it. It had an element of horror or spook, a quality that could not be defined that made you feel uneasy.

Daniel turned to me, piqued in interest.

"A tattoo?" he examined my bare arms, quickly surveying the nakedness of my skin.

"Didn't take you for the type, despite the Shovel." He gestured his head to the shop downstairs, and my bike resting in its place.

"What am I supposed to look like, then?" I poked, my voice full of a smile. I looked down at myself, exaggerating my gaze.

"Well, for starters, tattooed!" he shot back. "You're pretty clean-cut there, Annalise. That is not such a bad thing, either."

"I'm just full of surprises, I guess," the tone of my voice lowering. I rubbed my leg to wake the kitsune.

"So, tell me, what's a gal like you getting tattooed, then?" with genuine interest in his voice.

"A heron," I stated, matter-of-factly.

"The bird?" he replied.

"Ha, yup. The bird." Reaching out, I placed my mug on the edge of the plywood table.

I stretched for my bag with the cardboard tube secured to its front and shook the tube free. Working the drawings out of the cylinder, I leafed through the edges of the translucent papers until I spotted the wingtip of the heron. Pulling it free, I placed the rest of the drawings on the table. Holding the stencil to my chest over my shirt, I looked up to Daniel's gaze as he watched the bird's span crest shoulder to shoulder on my narrow body. He leaned in closer and examined the dynamism of the drawing.

"Wow," he said with sincerity. "It's incredible. You draw that?" He met my eyes.

"No, no, I didn't. My husband did." It became easier to say this time. He nodded, not looking for any more details on Dylan.

"It's intense and elegant," he remarked after a long pause.

I pulled the drawing from my chest and turned it so I could examine the lines.

"I'm a heron," I explained, with no further remarks to contextualize my comment.

Lying back, I rested my head on the pillow behind me and curled my feet up into a teepee on the cushion between us.

"You know what I dig about birds, about birds like the heron?" Daniel replied after a few minutes of silence. "They're present in three elements. Water, Air, and Earth. Think about it, that's rare." He nodded, agreeing with his own comment.

"They can glide between situations, environments, places, time . . . Pretty powerful creature if you ask me. They cross into spaces, and they, you know, they adapt." He ran his fingers behind his ears out of habit even though his hair sat already tucked in tightly.

I closed my eyes and imagined the heron's wingspan shrouding my body, feeling the flap of its energy keeping me cool. Everything you know of someone else is simply a construct of who you are, in the moment you share that particular experience with them. The moment that needle hits your skin is either relief or a violent stab; it is execution and liberation. When you connect with someone else, will it last in their skin too? Will it sink beneath the dermis and stay forever in the light, or will it be easily washed away at the first touch of water? The moment will age, the memory will age, the person will age, but none at the same rate, and it won't be the same experience for the two people that shared this moment.

Often, they are loneliest together. You bear this time as a single being bound as one; your pain becomes entwined, and you cannot tell what end of the needle you are on. You are either pushing it into another that you love or receiving it quietly and asking for more. You are not connected by the good that you have shared. You are tethered to each other so tightly by the pain of the needle dragging down your skin, by the pain of every lash, burn, and scar that has marked your soul. You can show these wounds to each other, accept them, kiss them, lick them, and run your healing hands over them to save them from having to look down and see the damage first-hand.

With my eyes still closed, I felt Daniel's body move, and his hand found mine. He gently held the tips of my fingers; a current crossed between us. I relaxed and squeezed him gently in thanks. We laid like this, still and lost in our own thoughts.

CHAPTER 25

When I awoke in the morning, Daniel had already started in the shop. I looked around the living room in the light of the morning. Every item where I'd left it, the heron drawing curled up on the floor next to me.

I swung my legs off the edge of the futon and stretched. Reaching for the drawing, I carefully curled it back into place in the center of the tube and gathered my belongings. After quickly washing my face and dressing, I was ready for the road again.

Lacing my boots and pulling on my jacket, I reached for the book once again before leaving. I knew the line I searched for by heart, somewhere in Chapter Two. I flipped to the section and began to scan the sentences, my eyes bouncing off the paragraphs in hunt for the words that were burned into my mind. Found them. *"And it occurred to me there is no manual that deals with the real business of motorcycle maintenance, the most important aspect of all. Caring about what you are doing is considered either unimportant or taken for granted."*

I reached for the mug of red wine left from the night before and dunked my pinky into the remaining liquid. I ran my finger around this quote, dipping it again and again to complete a crude oval. Tearing a tiny triangle off the bottom right corner of the page, I used it as a bookmark, sticking above the spine like a miniature sail in the distance on the horizon. I closed the book tightly around the marker and returned it to its home on the shelf.

I found Daniel on the shop floor leaning over a cluttered workbench in concentration, cleaning a small cylindrical engine part that I could not identify.

"Morning," he offered, not looking up.

"Hey, thanks again, Daniel. I mean it," I blushed, feeling out of place.

"Don't mention it." He was relaxed in his tone.

"What do I owe you?" I questioned, gesturing at the bike and the repair.

"Don't worry about it. Just be sure to stop in some time on your way through and show me that bird once it's done." He grinned at me over his shoulder.

"Ha, okay, deal," I said, shaking my head and touching the end of the tube housing the drawings grasped tightly in my hand.

I loaded my gear back onto the bike, and I pulled my helmet over my head. Releasing the kickstand, I fired up the Shovelhead and felt the familiar burping and gurgling of the powerful engine running through my hands. I backed the bike up, made a three-point turn, and looked over to Daniel with a nod. He walked to the garage door and pulled the heavy chain to raise the door for me. I gave the bike a push with my feet, walking it to the edge of the shop's threshold.

"Goodbye, my bird," Daniel smiled, calling over the roar of the motor.

I pulled lightly on the throttle and turned into the alley, lowering my left hand and pointing to the ground to wave farewell.

CHAPTER 26

$\mathcal{I}$ arrived in Reno at midday, the sun hot on my chest.

Reno sits high in the Nevada desert but is nestled in a valley and the Truckee River flows through town. Virginia Street, the main drag through town, was crowned by an arch that read *Reno, The Biggest Little City in the World*. The arch sat low over the street's entrance and shone gilded in glitter and vintage script. Casinos lined the street. The Atlantis, Harrah's, and the Silver Legacy all passed in my view as I slowed my bike down to crawl along with traffic. The sidewalks were scattered with pedestrians, and business' signs cluttered the landscape on both sides of me.

My eyes scanned the street numbers, hunting for the shop. It lived on the main drag; the sign caught my eye from a distance: *The Divorce Company Tattoo* scrolled across the glass in gold leaf.

A fellow motorbike was parked out front, leaving enough room for my Shovel. I pulled alongside it and turned the key, slipping my helmet off and my backpack on in a single, smooth motion. The front of the building appeared to be made of fine beige stucco, and flecks of dirt splatter up the bottom of the building where it met the sidewalk.

A calm propelled me forward; the nerves I'd felt at Teddy's shop were not there. Passing a young man smoking outside the entrance, I nodded, grasped the tube of drawings in my hands, and swung open the front door.

The same familiar scene, artwork, smells, and people filled the space as I approached the desk. This was a street shop, the sounds coming from the stations behind the partition were familiar: voices, music, laughter, and machines running up and down in unintentional harmony.

"I'm looking for Kirstin, please," I spoke with confidence.

"She's tattooing, can I help ya?" the young girl with stretched earlobes and a cut-off shop tshirt offered in a warm voice. She had piercings in her cheeks where dimples would sit, pulling in when she smiled.

"I'm hoping to book an appointment with her. A chestpiece." I gestured to my breastbone, running my hand across between my shoulders.

"She's booked up a couple of months out. What days work for you? We can take a look in her book," she replied, reaching for the appointment book and turning to the current week.

I had not considered this could happen, but I should have. Few tattooers are available the day you walk in; Teddy happened to be available because Teddy doesn't book clients anymore. A warm heat ran up my neck and over my cheeks. I should have called ahead, but I didn't know I was coming.

"I, um, I'm from up north, just coming through town quickly. Actually, just coming to town specifically to see

Kirstin. Is there any way I could just talk to her for five minutes?" I begged.

"She takes consults on Mondays from nine to eleven. Do you want to come back then?" She shifted her weight between her feet behind the desk, showing me impatience.

"I'll be gone by then. Is it okay if I just wait until she has a break?" I questioned, trying to make my voice mellowed and low.

"One sec." She pushed herself away from the counter and disappeared behind the curtained wall.

I could hear low voices and machines humming out of sync. She reemerged.

"Okay, Kirstin said to just have a seat and wait, and she'll come out on her break and talk." She gestured her chin over to a Victorian settee covered in dusty-rose velvet along the wall.

Placing my hand flat on the counter, I found her eyes, "Thank you, seriously."

I turned and tip-toed over to the seat, ensuring not to make any noise, and placed myself against the arm in the corner. I reached for the top portfolio from a pile on the table at my knees and laid it flat on my lap.

I turned the black plastic cover page open. The first image that stared back at me, a sketch on stencil paper, in red pencil, was a geisha with a fan spread over her face, revealing her eyes. Ornate beading dangled from her perfectly constructed hair, and powerful lines drew tiny cherry blossom patterns across her kimono. I held her gaze for a full minute, watching her tease the page. I traced my finger around her silhouette through the thin plastic protector and felt at ease.

The next page held a drawing of a crane perched in the water with tall patterned grass surrounding its body. Each feather was drawn with a geometric patterning that made up the details, and an upside-down skull stealthy hidden into the end of each feather, subtly staring back at me. Graphic water curled around the bird, making a frame, as if cut from a wooden block and rolled through a press; each finger wave formed into a perfect set.

Her drawings were clean, concise, and powerful. They looked like designs cut from origami paper with a precise hand and pieced together. There were blossoms and branches and waves on each page. There were fine dots and lines that looked machine-crafted, no hint of a human. Lily pads in sequence fitted together with snakes made of the negative space to create sculptured images tangled in perfect symmetry. Each drawing richer and more detailed than the next, visual fabrics and systematic elements crafted in place to fill the pages.

Growing anxious while waiting, I worried that she would not be able to tattoo me. I worried that my showing up unannounced would ruin my chances of sitting in her chair. Tilting my head back to rest on the rounded wooden trim of the sofa, I closed my eyes and sucked air in through my nose, the details of the drawings dancing on the back of my eyelids.

CHAPTER 27

I held the bamboo stake steady in the site while Nonna tied the delicate green bean shoot into place with a short piece of twine. Her knuckles each had a bulb-like a tiny crocus pod protruding from every joint from years of usage. I could hear the labored breathing from her nose and mouth as we worked with our heads close together in silence. "You-a know what the green bean is-a, Bella?" Nonna asked me, not looking up from her task.

"Like a vegetable, you mean?" I replied with question in my voice. I didn't understand.

"No, you know what God think the green bean is? He-a think it's the resurrection of Jesus Christ," raising her thumb to her lip and making the sign of the cross quickly over her closed mouth.

A loud and sharp laugh escaped my lips.

"Jesus is not a green bean, Nonna!" Laughter took over and shook my shoulders as I giggled.

"No, Bella!" Nonna replied sharply, not pleased with my laughter in reference to the Lord's name.

"I-a mean that the green beanstalk climbs up from the earth. It-a rise up and reach for heaven," she said, tilting her eyes up to the sky.

"It was the Greco people that-a tell me this on the boat when we-a come over from the Old Country together; we-a sit for five-a days on the boat and they-a tell me; they all-a bring their bean pods to make the seeds. That-a where these-a beans come-a from. I get them on the boat." She gestured at the vibrant green stalks with tiny curls shooting off in every direction.

"The Greco tell-a me that they are-a magic from their Gods. They use-a the bean to make the exorcism in the house. They make the ghosts and spirits leave the house." She never kidded with me. She was telling me the truth.

"When I get the-a *fagiolo* on-a the boat, it-a come in my dream every night for one-a week." She raised her pointer finger to show me the number one. Dirt was stuck to the skin, and she wore a watch with a thin gold strap made of elastic with a tissue stuck underneath it.

"I do not know do I plant the bean, or do I eat the bean!" she chuckled, and I relaxed.

"Every year, I-a plant the beans, and I-a harvest the beans." She swept her arm in front of us, gesturing at the patch.

"I-a keep five pods to-a dry and I put them in a jar under the sink" My brow stitched together at this comment, waiting. "I keep one-a pod for each my-a familia and make sure they are safe, so if I need to make the ghosts get out of the house, I can do it." She closed the conversation and kept tying tight knots onto the stake.

We continued to work our way down the narrow row in the garden, tying the green shoots to the supporting sticks, building a protective fence of green beans to block the house off from the danger and make our secret protective wall from the ghosts, keeping the world out.

CHAPTER 28

"Hey."

My head snapped up off the edge of the sofa, emerging from a trance.

Opening my eyes, a woman stood before me. Tight blue jeans, a black tank top, and worn black boots. She wore a pair of thick-rimmed glasses, and her hair was dyed a velvet black so dark it looked blue in the light. Short, poker-straight bangs framed across her forehead. Tattoos covered both arms, running down her hands and patterning her fingertips. Her nails were filed to points and glossed in an ebony paint. A large moth spanned across her chest, touching each shoulder and disappearing into her shirt. Her frame was light and lean, and looked much younger than I expected.

"Kirstin," she offered, reaching out her hand to shake mine.

I jumped to my feet, "Annalise." Her fingers were warm and firm.

"Thanks for seeing me. Sorry I didn't book a consult."

"Hey, I get it. You're passing through?" she nodded her chin at my bike out front, her eyes training over my leather jacket.

"Yeah, sort of," I replied, not knowing where I was going.

"So, what is it you're looking to do?" she lifted her hand from her side, suggesting we return to the sofa.

We sat, and I pulled the roll of drawings from the tube in my lap, freeing the coiled papers. I leafed through the edges, spotted the tip of the heron's wing, and pulled it free from the swirled pile.

Spreading the paper out over the black portfolios in front of us, we leaned over the drawings and I watched as Kirstin examined the sketch.

"Where did this come from?" she questioned gently, not taking her eyes away from the bird.

"My husband drew it," I stated. "His name was Dylan." The words were much easier to say than I expected.

She nodded slowly, acknowledging the tense without asking further questions.

"This isn't really my style, Annalise," Kirstin offered. "What is it you want done with it?" being kind, and patiently waiting for my reply.

"Well, I'm hoping you can take this drawing and make it yours," I replied, reaching for the drawing and holding it up to my chest.

"I want to place it here, but I'm hoping you can turn it into one of your stylized pieces, total freedom to change it up." I glanced at the portfolio; she knew what I was getting at.

She silently waited for a long while, staring through the drawing, through my chest, looking past my ribs and into my flesh. My heartbeat red and blue and pulsing with blood; oxygen rushing to the organ as it pumped and pumped. She watched my heart beating for a full minute, drawing the tattoo with her mind as the blood circulated through my organs.

"Okay, I will see what I can do. It's elegant right like it is; I almost hate to touch it."

She spoke with honesty, being respectful.

"Dylan would be proud to have you add to it," I said, smiling, knowing it to be true.

"I'm scared to ask, but when do you think you could fit me in?" my voice rising as the thought trailed off.

She glanced up to the clock that hung over the door. A sign perched under it that said MY MOM & GOD GET TATTOOED FOR FREE, EVERYONE ELSE PAYS CASH.

"Can you come back in the morning, say nine o'clock?" her voice sounded uncertain.

"Yeah, wow, for sure. Kirstin, seriously, thank you for fitting me in!" A smile took over my face, surprised.

"Hey, don't mention it. Next time, just book ahead!" She smirked.

I bowed my head dramatically, in thanks. With that, I rolled up the remaining drawings and put them into the tube, walking over to the front counter. I pulled a small roll of cash from my pocket that had been secured with an elastic from one of Dylan's machines, just as he always did. I grabbed a hundred-dollar bill from the roll and pushed it across the counter.

"My deposit." I nodded.

The young woman pulled the bill from the counter and placed it in the back of the appointment book.

"Your name?" she asked.

"Annalise. I will be back tomorrow morning at nine."

I turned to the door and pushed out into the warmth.

CHAPTER 29

I had tossed and turned all night in the motel room off Virginia Street. A tidy time warp from the 1970s with golden carpet, heavy burnt orange drapes, and a tube television perched in the corner. When the alarm rang at 7:00 a.m., I was already awake and staring into the minuscule gold flecks sprayed into the popcorn texture on the ceiling. They caught the first of the morning sun sneaking in through a crack in the curtains.

I stretched my toes and pushed my arms into the air, allowing the tension of the movement to take over my body. Turning onto my side, I fixed my gaze on the roll of drawings, knowing that the heron was missing, being kept safe by Kirstin at the shop overnight.

My feet touched the carpet as I swung my legs over the bed and dug my toes into the rough Berber. Slowly rising, I felt calm, but a course of fear came through my body.

"Dylan," I whispered, my lips barely making a shape to let his name out. "You're a crow."

Tears welled up in my eyes as I thought of the woman on the floor in The Easel, telling me the story of the resting hunter. My mind closed around the single letter he'd tattooed on his wrist, the capital A that pointed at me and pierced my skin when he offered his arm to me to see it. An arrowhead with a finely sharpened tip aimed at the sky, searching for a heron. I put my thumb over my wrist where he'd tattooed the initial and pressed my nail into the flesh until it stung. I repeated this with my nail until I'd made an arrow shape, and crossed the center to form a crude A. Raising my wrist up in the air, I closed one eye to look down my arm, taking aim with my arrow. With that, I stood and prepared for the day.

I pulled my shirt, bra, and underwear from the shower rod where I'd hung them the night before after washing them in the avocado-green sink. They were covered in fine wrinkles from wringing out the water by hand, twisting the fabric until my knuckles whitened. The panties and bra were still slightly damp around the trim, and I smoothed the t-shirt over my head, ignoring the creases that traveled diagonally across its surface.

First, I scrubbed my face in the sink, then I brushed my teeth and pulled my hair into a low ponytail to ensure it would fit under my helmet. As I stood over the vanity, I stopped and followed my eyes in the mirror. I touched my cheeks and ran my fingers down the bridge of my nose and across my lips. Spreading my arms out to my sides, I flapped them like wings, once, twice, three times. With that, I spun on my heel to find my pants and bag, and then load up my bike.

CHAPTER 30

Outside of the shop, the sidewalk looked dusty, and cigarette butts littered the pathway. As I approached the door a movement caught the corner of my eye a few feet away, and I jumped. Turning to look, I saw a small dog with a whiskery face, muzzle full of grey. It was missing a leg but balanced on three without any trouble. Squatting down, I whistled through my teeth; it hesitated and delicately pranced over, using three legs in a close-knit pattern to move quickly to me.

He sniffed my outstretched hand, and his coarse tongue licked my wrist. He sat in front of me with an uncomfortable space where his front leg should be as I stared at him. Suddenly, he hopped up and ran off down the street, a practiced hobble that involved a skip and a jump to complete the stride.

He turned a corner and was gone.

Entering the shop, I saw the air filled with dust particles as the sun followed me inside.

My eyes adjusted to the room, and I scratched my scalp to relieve the pressure from my helmet.

Kirstin appeared in the doorway, smiling with a paper cup of coffee in her hand.

"Morning, Annalise," she welcomed me, adrenaline filling my limbs.

"Hi," I offered back, raising my hand in a static wave. It was still early; no other tattooers or patrons had arrived yet.

"Come on back," she instructed, tilting her head over her shoulder to show the way.

Behind the curtained front entrance lived an open studio with four stations, all silent; tools cleaned and perched waiting for the tattooers to arrive later that day. I followed her to the back corner station on the right, near the only window in the room. I could see the bed draped and inks set out and waiting in their capsules to begin.

"I hope you like what I did with the drawing," she said.

The translucent stencil paper was laid out over the bed, edges curling and moving like tree leaves in the air. I approached the drawing with hesitation, trying not to look down until fully positioned in front of it and viewing it from its intended angle. My eyes scanned wing to wing the ornate pattern and shape of the bird—every inch of the stencil filled with mazes, shapes, geometries, and details.

An Escher illustration inside of a living creature, my eyes twisted through the layers that formed the bird's powerful physique. She'd maintained the integrity of the drawing; I could see Dylan's hand that guided the outline and the dynamism of the creature, but she'd embedded tiny blocks and patterns in each section.

The wings were made of individual feathers, each deeply embellished with crossed lines and at the tip of each wing, an upside-down letter *D*. The chest of the bird curled under the drawing, the curved lines each looking like strings lined up next to one another, creating a three-dimensional cage. The tail swooped behind the drawing, taking the perspective off into the distance. The feathers created a Japanese fan, wallpapers of ornamented designs filled every plume.

The creature's head appeared bold and dark, nearly filled in completely with solid black. The features and lines of the beak and eye were in negative space, the beak perched open, and a flower carried in its mouth. She'd added this in; a filigreed marigold with a single leaf holding onto the stem. The delicate turns of each petal forcing your eye to its center. The heron clutched a necklace in its talons made of fine chain, blowing in the wind created by flight; the charm of a tiny bird's skull, its beak turned down. I imagined it to be the skull of a crow.

Reaching for the paper, I ran my fingers over the swooping line of *D*s formed in the plumage of the wings and let them trace over the diminutive skull charm. My eyes met Kirstin's and no words came to my mouth, even though I opened my lips and tried to speak.

"You like it, then?" she questioned.

"I want to wear this," I replied, not knowing how else to express myself and feeling cheesy for saying that.

"Okay, then. I will take that as a yes!" She laughed and began moving into her ritual of motions, setup, and preparation.

As she fit the stencil together, I removed my top and sat on the edge of the bed, watching her work. I examined myself in the mirror behind her, picturing the heron's powerful wings stretched across my chest. I grinned at the thought of hiding this mortal under my clothing each day; my fingers traced my collar bone.

She walked over to me with the stencil, the purple dye glowing through the thin paper, and held it up by each wingtip across my chest. Her head tilted side to side as she made slight adjustments to the angle before walking back to her station and cutting around the edges with scissors.

I stood as she approached me, her hands shrouded in black gloves. I pulled my bra straps down my shoulders to drape around my arms. She marked down the center of my chest with a felt pen, the delicate wet tip tickling my skin. A dash of horizontal lines to be used as guides for placement. Her face creased deeply in concentration, the number eleven appearing in the folds of skin between her brows.

I stretched my neck slightly up to the ceiling, holding my breath to steady myself as she worked. As the stencil was laid on my skin with the liquid to transfer, it felt as if I had been covered in protective armor. The air stopped from reaching me, and the draped paper clung to my flesh. The sensation felt invigorating. I slowly rotated my shoulders to feel the wave of the stencil paper cross my body. Glancing down to see the purple ink of the stencil seeping through and blurring across the surface, I examined the fine details of the drawing bleeding together.

Kirstin took a step back and contemplated the placement. Satisfied, she stood to my side so I could watch my reflection as she peeled back the wrapping. The drawing made a mirror image as it released steadily from my skin; I watched it unfold like a Rorschach blot—the inner workings of a kaleidoscope being revealed in minuscule embellishments over my flesh.

The cool air rushed to my chest and clung to the gel. Walking closer to the mirror, I studied the placement. The tip of each wing curled perfectly over my shoulders, the talons clutching the charm dangling down my chest and resting hidden between my breasts.

"It's beyond what I imagined, Kirstin," I murmured, lost for an expression. I turned to her as her eyes flickered between the stencil and my gaze.

"Okay, lie down then and let's get started." Her hand patted the edge of the draped table.

I obliged and climbed up, laying on my back and closing my eyes.

Hearing the machine's power supply engage, my body tightened, knowing what was to come. I released the tension from my fingers and pressed my arms flat into the soft cushioned top of the table. As the needle first touched down and the tone of the hum deepened, I felt pain and relief and control.

"Tattooing takes patience," Kirstin offered me. "It's a process of getting hurt to be healed, I suppose. It takes hours, days, even years of suffering to finish a big project."

I knew she understood why I was here.

"You can learn how to overcome pain when the needle pierces you; you can steal its strength and step closer to being complete."

Opening my eyes, I looked down at her hand, the crown of her head, and felt her breath on my skin as she hovered close to my body.

"It's like you have a secret when you have a tattoo; you get to capture its power, house it privately, and release it only when you want to. When you need to. In the time it takes you to complete a big piece, you mature, you change, you age. You grow."

Drinking in her words, I let a stream of slow air release from my lips. I've heard this before.

My chest felt completely numb, and the pain vibrated through my body; the pain on the chest was far worse than the hip—no cushion between the needle and my bones. I pictured each nerve ending jumping to attention, and gritted my teeth. Sweat collected on my back. I waited for her next thought. The room fell quiet and I listened to the buzz of her machines, waited for her to wipe my skin, to add another line, to move methodically across my body. I wanted her to stop, but I didn't ever want to leave this place.

"Full-time tattooer, part-time shrink, I suppose," she joked, lightening her thoughts and the mood of the room.

I flinched. She felt me shift. My body, my temperature. The intensity worsened on my chest; I wasn't prepared for how much this would hurt. Breathing deeply through my nose, I steeled my mind to the pain. I welcomed it.

"Do you know about the name of my shop here?" she inquired, changing the subject.

"No, no clue," I answered with honesty.

"Well, Reno used to be the easiest state to get a divorce in the early 1930s. To boost the economy during the Great Depression, they let people come to the state for a quickie separation!" Her voice was animated; she'd told this story before.

"You set up camp here for six weeks, and they'd let you split the sheets," she chuckled, her machine not stopping while she spoke.

"Rita Hayworth, Norman Rockwell, and Bugsy Siegel all came here to get divorces. That's why there are all these resorts and luxury hotels from that era. You'd come here, take a vacation, and leave single after waiting out your six-week stay as a resident." She went silent, shaking her head at the thought.

"I had no idea," I responded.

"Yeah, you had to have someone be 'guilty' to get the papers put through until the 60s," she continued on. "Like, I mean, you had to have a plaintiff, someone had to be in the wrong before you'd be allowed to leave them. Can you imagine? You had to have proof!" her tone very playful.

Proof that you're unhappy.

"The year before the war, Reno married 25,000 people. The year after the war, they divorced 10,000. Probably half of the same folks." She scoffed, punctuating her comment. "Fault and guilt, you had to have fault and guilt to split up. Can you imagine?"

I could not. I could not imagine having to prove fault and guilt to leave Dylan. Or to have Dylan leave me. Divorce would have been harder than his death, I thought. Culpability riddled my body with that thought. Admitting failure would have been more shameful than being a widow. I felt sick at this thought, and too pathetic to speak it out loud.

"Have you ever been married?" I inquired, trying to redirect my thoughts.

"Just to my shop. Just to this machine, and my drawing table, and my clients."

Her comment resonated with me; I understood that more than she could comprehend.

"You can only love tattooing. You can't love a person and love tattooing, unfortunately. She's a full-time mistress."

Her words measured, the thrum of her machine pacing along my dermis.

Hours had passed. Kirstin had me move to face my head at the other end of the table to reach my opposite shoulder. She stood, stretched, and laid out a fresh drape; blood, fluid, sweat, ink, and wash smeared together and made watercolor puddles over the light blue paper. I wondered how many times Kirstin had rolled up a drop cloth with the evidence of a person's tattoo and thrown it away. *Thousands?*

Lying back down onto the fresh sheet, I prepared for the needle to touch my skin again. I didn't look in the mirror or down at my chest while we repositioned, wanting to take it in all at once.

"I never thought of coming to Reno before last week," I blurted out. "I didn't know I needed this until last week, and then I had to have it more than anything in the world. My bike broke down, and I thought that was the end of it. I cried on the side of the road like a schoolgirl over it." I snickered with embarrassment.

"Do you like it here so far?" Kirstin prodded.

"I don't know," I answered frankly. "Most days, I wake up and I don't know what I like anymore. I don't know what feels good. I only know that these last two weeks are the first time I've felt awake in months. I can see and hear and smell. I feel something. A lot of it feels pretty bad to be honest, but I feel it and that means I'm better." I held my breath, waiting for her to reply, for her to probe, but she didn't say a word.

She knew that I wasn't looking for a response.

I felt the needle lift from my skin. Kirstin reached for the spray bottle, pulling a fresh paper towel from a neat pile at the side of her station. She lathered my raw chest and shoulders in moisture and wiped them down using full pressure. It burned, and felt like relief. She did it again and again. I knew this meant it was over. The shop began to fill with other artists, other clients. My private moment, gone.

"Well, Annalise, now that I'm done, I'll tell you I haven't been that stressed over a drawing since my apprenticeship. I wanted it to be everything you needed, and I hope it is."

Her gloved fingers rested on my shoulder lightly. She moved her hand away, and I knew it was my cue to sit up. My body felt exhausted, and my head felt light as I raised myself up.

I rubbed my hands along my thighs; the fox quickly awakened and waited to take in this new member. Turning to face the mirror, my eyes began to clear, and I became startled by the contrast of the black form against my white skin. My shoulders pressed back, and my chest became pert; the wings moved across my body as I pushed myself onto my feet and tentatively stepped toward the woman in the reflection.

Each stroke of the needle laid perfectly on my form, and the lines were bold, tight, and clean; Dylan's hand showing through in each powerful line, but not holding on too firmly. I wanted to touch the heron, run my hands over her wings and stroke her face, but I resisted. Instead, I turned to Kirstin and bowed my head.

"Thank you," I said to the floor, avoiding her eyes and avoiding a moment of intimacy that I knew I couldn't take right now.

"It's been my pleasure, Annalise. I hope Dylan would be happy with what I've done to it."

Her tone was tentative and gentle at the mention of his name.

"Dylan was more of a crow; I'm a heron."

Kirstin nodded, following, but not understanding. She began to clean her station and let me stand and examine myself in the mirror. The shop had begun to fill up and other tattooers and patrons moved about the space, laughing, talking, and working. The sounds they made turned into the ocean pushing waves onto the shore, noise swelling and falling in sets.

She called for me, and I turned to see her prepared with bandages and tape to wrap the bird and hide her away.

"Where are you going now?" she inquired, her gloved hands working carefully to cover the bird tightly and seal the fresh wound off from outside forces.

Her eyes shot up and caught mine.

"I'm not sure where to go. I don't know who will be able to help me with this one other tattoo I need."

Need.

"What's it of?" she pressed.

"A Ganesh. He's beautiful, and traditional. He'll go on my thigh." It became easier to talk about collecting work now; I felt like I had earned credits.

"You trying to stay local?" she questioned further, her mind reviewing the Rolodex of tattooers that could accomplish this design.

I smirked. "I have no idea where 'local' is."

"Do you have your passport?" she smiled.

Finished bandaging the tattoo, her hands rested on my shoulders. It felt safe.

"Yes, I do. Kirstin, where are you sending me?" I giggled, it felt like I had a friend.

I understood why Dylan's clients all thought they had a connection.

"I'll call ahead for you and arrange an appointment," she replied.

"Follow me out front. We'll settle up and I will get you the address."

Excitement entered my body. I felt awake.

CHAPTER 31

*F*all had turned to winter, and winter had slowly passed. Spring settled in. Nonna had pruned the garden, unwrapped the tomato plants, and cleared the ground of the layers of newspaper and dried leaves she had used to protect her soil from the season that was behind us now. I'd be turning sixteen in a few days, and Nonna had begun to talk about my upcoming day with each visit, preparing foods and pastries, and discussing the cake she would bake me.

"*Sedici*, my God," she whispered, raising her gold crucifix to her lips and kissing it lightly, as I passed her on my way to the bathroom in her narrow hallway.

I prepared to begin my freshman year in high school and was in front of the mirror in the bathroom examining the thin, wiry hairs that had sprouted under my arms.

"*Sedici*, Nonni. I'm old enough to drive. Maybe you can take me!" I joined her again in the kitchen where she worked over the counter rolling out a long string of dough to make tradalli for morning coffee.

She chuckled. "No, no, Bella. Nonno would have-a take-a you for the drive. I bake."

I'd never seen her drive before, but she loved to tell me about learning to drive a standard transmission in the Old Country with her Papa.

"Nonna, what will happen to me this year?" A question I'd been asking her for as long as I could remember on my birthday.

While she was a fiercely religious woman, she believed in the magic of astrology when it came to one's birthday, though she'd never admit it.

"God will show us his plan for-a you," she returned quickly, without hesitation. "I will get the book, *aspettare*," waving her hand.

The book was a finely printed soft-covered volume that she kept in her dresser drawer. It was made of pages thinner than onion skins and had a wine-colored plastic cover. The print was in Italian, and I couldn't understand the words, but there were pictures every so often. Stamped on the cover in embossed gold letters, it read *Aprile*. April. The month I had been born.

"Nonna, where did this book even come from?" I questioned, never having bothered to ask before.

"It was-a gift from my neighbor from-a when you were born," she replied.

"Sit," she commanded, perched at the round kitchen table.

Her fingers found the page she'd been searching for, dog-eared. Her crooked finger scanned along the lines, looking for the section she needed to answer my questions.

"Well, Bella. It-a gonna be some good and some very bad."

Her eyes found mine, her lower lids rimmed with red. My hands went still.

"Bad?" I asked. She'd never read me bad news from this book on my birthday before.

"Your birth chart tell-a me, Bella. This year, you must learn to cope with death," she clutched at the cross hanging from the chain on her neck and raised it to her lips again.

"You are a *Toro*, a strong bull, Bella. That means death will come to your home."

Her eyes searched the page, the text, the delicate chart.

"*Si*, Bella. Death this year on the chart. Not for-a you. But close to you. *Morte*."

Matter-of-factly is how she delivered this to me; my head spun at the thought. Nonna traced her finger around the wheel on the center of the page, tapping a pie-shaped slice of the diagram.

"This is-a you, Rising Sun. I know you-a stubborn bull and you do not want to believe what I tell you, Bella."

Her hand reached over and gripped my forearm with unexpected strength. "It best not to know when the reaper come."

She raised a crooked finger to her lips and kissed it while looking up to God.

With that, she pushed herself back from the table and swept the book under her arm, making her way back to the counter.

"You want-a chocolate or you want vanilla for your *torta* this year, Bella?" she inquired, as if the discussion had never happened.

CHAPTER 32

*M*y bike carried me back north. She climbed out of the Nevada desert with ease, turning into the shadows and bringing cooler air along with her. I was comfortable with her now, riding with one hand tucked into the crease at my hip, the other holding the throttle. My feet rested on the highway pegs where the road straightened, and the vibration of the motor below me brought a meditative effect that I never understood until now.

Dylan riding his bike away from the house sprung to mind, escaping with the therapeutic numbing of the trembling engine. The address of the shop Kirstin was sending me to was written on a corner of tracing paper in red pencil crayon. I'd tucked it into the breast pocket of my jacket, snug against the heron. My mind imagined the heron's wings spreading wide and catching the wind as I rode north. The bike seemed to be pointed home, but we were not heading that way.

Mountains began to form around me, building up shadows in the landscape and casting dark pools over the road's surface. I thought to *Zen and the Art of Motorcycle Maintenance* and finally understood his passage about mountains, suddenly relevant. Suddenly, it meant everything.

"Mountains should be climbed with as little effort as possible and without desire. The reality of your own nature should determine the speed. If you become restless, speed up. If you become winded, slow down. You climb the mountain in an equilibrium between restlessness and exhaustion. Then, when you're no longer thinking ahead, each footstep isn't just a means to an end but a unique event in itself . . . To live only for some future goal is shallow. It's the sides of the mountains which sustain life, not the top."

I was no longer in a hurry to run away and grasp for the next feeling of happiness, or to get to the top of the mountain. The hedonic treadmill had begun to fade, and the sides of the mountains came into focus. I flexed my arms and gripped the handlebars tightly as I rode deeper into the mountain's gap and let the darkness follow behind me. My body became a ghost, and the bike drove itself without resistance, north, north.

The sharp wind numbed my face, and I welcomed it, feeling every sensation the mountains wanted to bring to me. I'd found the perfect speed, between restlessness and exhaustion. Every minute that passed marked the start of a new opportunity. As I collected the minutes in silence with the bike rumbling underneath me, a slight shock in what I was doing registered. I sat up taller.

My mind wandered to Dylan, sitting at his drawing table at the house, remembering him drawing the feathers of a bird. Dylan had tattooed the mighty phoenix rising from the ashes dozens of times. The powerful bird circled in oranges, golden yellows, and reds. Its graceful wings in the action of taking off from the ground, swirling its tail feathers into the flames.

"I'm tired of tattooing this fucken bird," he'd grumbled to me, hunched over his drawing table at the house preparing the stencil for the next day.

"Really?" taken aback, surprised at the comment. Birds were always a favorite of his to draw and tattoo.

"Yeah, every recovering addict, every single mom, every bored white girl that thinks her life has been hard needs to get a phoenix rising from the ashes and tell me all about their transformation," his voice dripped with sarcasm, waving his hands in the air while he spoke.

"I don't fucken care," he said to himself, returning his pencil back to the stencil paper.

"You're not a phoenix. No one is a phoenix. You're a fucken loser."

I turned and stared at him for a long while. I watched the slope of his shoulder as he swept his hand over the page, roughing in the gesture of flames.

"I don't even know where the image of the phoenix rising from the ashes even comes from. Is it the bible?" My voice got very high, afraid of sounding stupid.

"Nah," he answered patiently.

Relief filled my limbs.

"It's this mythical bird, and it lives for like a hundred years or something, really old. Its tail feathers are made of fire. When it's ready to die, it goes to its nest and burns up the nest and itself."

He turned to face me, pressing the palm of his hand into his knee.

"The twigs and the bird burn down to ash, and from the ashes, a reborn phoenix rises up." His hand swam up in the air, passing his face like a jellyfish.

The mythology lesson ended, and he turned back to his table.

Suffer through your own demise, and you, too, shall rise up.

The sun had gotten low, and the sky appeared licked with the fiery colors of the phoenix's tail feathers, the burning plumage sweeping the edges of the mountains as far as my eyes could see. I rode into the nest.

CHAPTER 33

*T*hree days had passed, and I'd reached the border. Crossing into Canada, I'd sat on my bike, waiting in a lineup of cars crossing into British Columbia. After passing through the security check and passport reviews, the agent stared me down, examining my eyes.

"What's your business in Canada, Ma'am?"

Ma'am. The word took me aback; I felt like a Miss.

"Um, ah, I'm heading to Vancouver to get a tattoo." Nerves shook me, I felt guilty, but there was no crime, aside from riding without a license.

"And how long will you be staying?" he asked. His eyes were hidden behind dark shades that wrapped around the sides of his face.

"A night or two, I suppose," I hadn't given it any thought.

"Do you have any weapons on you? Alcohol, tobacco, or any gifts that will be left behind in the country?" A script he'd run through many times.

"No, sir," I replied. I felt sweat forming inside my gloved hands.

"Any citrus fruit? Meat?" I smiled, thinking it seemed obvious that I didn't have much room to carry perishable goods.

"No, sir. Just myself and a change of clothes or two."

He walked to the back of my bike and looked around from a distance.

"Okay, ma'am. Enjoy your trip." His hand outstretched, returning my passport to me.

I reached for it and tucked it into my breast pocket with the shop address. I pulled my helmet and glasses back on, and fired up the engine, riding off.

Following the highway signs, I steered to the ocean, traffic tightening across the lanes as we neared the heart of the city. The city glowed, each pane of glass cladding on the tall buildings reflecting the warm aqua light of the ocean's surface. People lined the streets; the sidewalks were full. Buses clogged the right-hand lane, and traffic crawled along as pedestrians crossed the street at each intersection.

I was looking for The Frenchy. When Kirstin told me the name of the shop she was sending me to, I smirked. Dylan loved the story of the Flying Frenchy and often talked about its lore. I remembered him telling me that people confused The Frenchy shop name with the story of The Flying Frenchy, but they weren't related. He loved to bring this detail up when people got it wrong, to flex his knowledge. The Frenchy was quite literally that, a French man.

The Flying Frenchy was a legendary ghost ship that, no matter the effort, could never make it to port. Damned to sail the oceans forever, it was perpetually lost at sea. Sightings were recorded in the nineteenth and twentieth centuries. The ship had been described as glowing with ghostly light. A small oil painting of it hung in Dylan's station at the tattoo shop, burnt umber and ochre radiating from the ship's bow.

It was said that The Flying Frenchy could communicate with the dead, and if a passing ship spotted the phantom vessel on the open seas, it was bound for doom itself.

"Don't look at it for too long, Annalise," Dylan snickered when he first hung the painting in its place.

"Why not?" I teased back.

"If you try to communicate with the Flying Frenchy, ye will be bound for ruins," he chuckled in a pirate's voice, and I looked down at the floor.

I saw the sign for the shop as I approached and felt surprised, taken aback by its modest exterior—a long, narrow, in-filled space made of cement blocks. A few stairs led up to a single door with metal bars on the tall window to its left. A hand-painted sandwich board rested on the sidewalk outside that read *The Frenchy*, in cursive script. It looked old and weathered. A metal hand-railing leading up the stairs was once painted bright yellow but now had been pitted heavily with rust from the wet, salty air.

The same familiar sounds and smells filled my senses as I entered the shop. Every inch of wall space in the waiting area was completely covered with framed flash, and a large Japanese fan spanned across the back wall. The shop seemed busy; I could hear machines running in and out of sync from behind the wall, voices and laughter escaping to the front of the house. An older woman sat behind the desk; her thick black hair braided down her back with streaks of grey showing at her temples. Her shirt appeared to be made of red satin, and small, white flowers were puckering the fabric where they were embroidered in place.

"Welcome," she offered softly with a deep and brief nod of the head.

Chills ran over my body. I felt a pang of wishing Dylan could experience this for the first time since I'd left home.

"Hey, I'm Annalise," I replied.

I raised my hand to my chest and spread my fingers across my heart, over the heron.

"I have an appointment with . . . with Clive. With The Frenchy. With Clive The Frenchy."

I suddenly felt silly not knowing what to call him.

Her face smiled, "Yes, of course you do. Clive is ready for you."

She turned her body to the side and gestured with her arm to follow her behind the large curtain. The fabric that hung from the doorway was made of two linen panels. It was a split dragon, one side in full color and the other side in black and grey. The colored side had chaos spinning around the drawing, its nostril flared and an eye staring straight ahead. The black and grey side hung in static, precise and almost welcoming. I parted the curtain with my hand, pulling back the ferocious side and flicking it over my shoulder as I passed through the mouth of the shop.

Clive was in his sixties, curls of grey hair framing his ears. A short-sleeve button-down shirt hung loosely on his lean frame. He stood and offered me his hand.

"Clive," he stated with confidence; his voice was very gentle and his movements were instantly soft.

"Annalise," I offered back, taking his outstretched hand into a firm shake.

"I've been waiting for you," said Clive with a very kind smile. He seemed unlike the other tattooers I'd known, light and seemingly wise. "Not much surprises me anymore, but this, this surprised me. Kirstin called out of the blue and said you were coming. I felt surprised in a good way," he finished his sentence with a broad smile, revealing square teeth that were grey on the edges.

I liked him.

"And you've come for a Ganesh. All tattooers as old as me love tattooing the Ganesh. This day is a gift, I suspect."

My eyes scanned his body, resting at the blurred blue ink dusting his knuckles. *HOLD FAST* it read, spread out over eight digits. Dylan's knuckles had said the same thing.

"You know the story of the Ganesh, I'm guessing?" Clive offered over his shoulder as we walked down the hall to his studio.

"I know the story of how he'd been created," I replied. "My husband was very interested in all of the gods. His bookshelves were lined with the drawings and folklore of the Ganesh, and lots of the other deities, actually."

The Ganesh was an elephant-headed boy in his final form. He began as an average boy, an only child to his parents, Shiva and Parvati, created by his mother Parvati, while his father Shiva had been away. I could see the story of the Ganesh in one of Dylan's favorite books. The page spread with a colorful drawing of the god, with a skinny column of text telling his story bracketing the right-hand side of the page. Ganesh had been guarding the door of his mother's home when his father arrived back home, not recognizing Ganesh. Refusing to let him pass, Shiva cut the head off the boy to get through the doors to his home. The head flew off the boy's body, and the body dropped to the floor.

Shiva realized he'd beheaded his own child after the distraught Parvati discovered what had happened, and he panicked and ran to the forest. He slayed the head off of an elephant and attached it to the boy's body to reincarnate him for his wife. He became loved by his parents, a god that should always be worshiped first.

"Well, I have him all drawn up for you, Annalise," Clive's voice was soft. He'd already prepared a stencil of his own, there was no need for me to get Dylan's drawing from the tube.

"Kirstin said you're a tough gal; you sat like a rock for her on that chest piece. This will be a piece of cake compared to that," he chuckled, knowing how sensitive the chest is to get tattooed. "It will just require patience. But what doesn't," he said.

"I'm ready," I replied, excitement in my voice.

The drawing hung pinned to the wall. I saw the elephant-boy's head as soon as I walked into the well-lit studio. His large head, powerful, outlined in thick and bold strokes, intimidating yet welcoming to look at—his oversized ears representative of his empathy, balanced by a small mouth. Dylan's book had taught me the symbolism for Ganesh's composition, and I had it memorized. He had a single broken tusk in Clive's rendering, just like in the book. It represented keeping the good and throwing away the bad, much like his rounded belly as a marker of consuming the good and bad in life.

I embraced the Ganesh with my gaze, searching for his four hands. They held a rope - to pull us forward toward our goals and realize ourselves - the next featured an axe, to cut off attachments. The third hand offered a dish of sweet treats to reward oneself for spiritual development, and the fourth hand was frozen in the position of the mudra. The mudra gesture offers a blessing for those that worship him.

His image had been created perfectly. Detailed and meticulously drawn, just the way Dylan would have wanted to see him. I could feel the hours Clive had poured into this drawing for me, for us.

"You know the Ganesh is a symbol of protection. He will keep you safe," he said and smiled.

I felt safe here.

"He shows us obstacles in life and tests us, and then he helps us remove those obstacles and lets us grow."

Our eyes met, and I nodded, knowing he understood my being here.

"You can overcome anything in life, Annalise. Ganesh is a simple teacher of just that."

He turned to the drawing and gave it a swift tug off the wall, where it was waiting held by a single pin.

CHAPTER 34

"Your book was right, Nonna," I whispered, my lips pressed against the crêpey and speckled skin on the back of her hand.

The hand that had stroked my hair, the hand that had cooked every meal for our family for as long as I could remember. The hand that planted the mums each year in the garden to keep the bugs away from the tomatoes. The hand that prayed.

She was lying on her back on her bed, the position she'd been in for days. Her breaths were very shallow, and I rubbed ice chips on her lips to soothe their red surface. Tears filled my throat, trying to will her back. I wanted to fix her, have her back in her apron, in the garden, in prayer, but I knew this moment was it. *Safortuna*. Bad luck. My shoes on the bed were the first step toward this; the book told us this would come, and I didn't want to believe it.

"Nonna."

I wanted her to reply, to whisper, "Bella."

Nothing. Just the tick of the small bedside clock on her nightstand.

"Don't leave me," I pleaded with her, a pointless request.

The year of turning sixteen had come true. Rising, I reached across her body to retrieve her worn bible lying by her side, rosary tangled on top. I slid the small card of Saint Francis from between the pages and tucked it into the waistband of my skirt; placing her bible back at her side, I rested her hand on top of it.

"*Ci sentiamo,* Nonna. I will see you in one hundred years." I buried my face in her warm hand, listening to the painful pattern of her lungs, counting each gasp.

CHAPTER 35

"The placement looks good to me," Clive said to himself.

I nodded.

He'd laid and relaid the stencil three times, looking for the perfect fit on my hip and thigh, my skin a smear of transparent purple stencil ink.

"I needed this side of the drawing to follow the curve of your body," he informed me, adding a few additional lines to the stencil on my skin with a felt pen.

I was not worried; I trusted his process and appreciated the attention he gave to me. Standing in front of him in my underwear and socks, I noticed his station waiting, set up neatly, each tool in its designated place. The Frenchy tattooed in a private room, away from the other tattooers at the shop. My eyes scanned over the inks, each brimming over the edge of the tiny caps they filled. The curve of the liquid sat just shy of the edge of the miniature cup. His machines were coil, as to be expected, each wrapped in a clear blue plastic bag along with the clip cord for protection. He pulled his gloves off and reached for a fresh pair.

He grabbed the liner off the work surface and released the needle from its place, then tipped it into the yellow sharps box placed on the floor. Clive reached for a new needle and freed it from the plastic packaging.

"I thought I wanted a seven, but I need a nine," he explained to me. "This Ganesh needs bolder lines. I want you to feel the impact when you look at it!" His voice moved, full of motion.

I nodded in response, grateful for his energy.

"Hop up," Clive commanded, reaching for his stool and tucking his knees under the edge of the table.

I obliged and walked the Ganesh up the steps of the temple and laid down.

Laying in silence for at least an hour, I listened to the nine-liner as it bored into my flesh. I felt such deep referral pains as he stroked the machine over my thigh that my foot tingled and reacted to the ache. My ears picked up the peal of the machine like a tuning fork ringing to the corners of the room.

"The machine has its own mantra," Clive said as if reading my mind.

"It does," I affirmed, his words breaking the continued wave of sound in the room.

"You know the mantra of the Ganesh?" he inquired.

"No, I don't." I turned my chin to him over my shoulder.

"You call Ganesh for happiness, success, luck, and beauty. You can use the chant however you want; there are no rules for his mantra." Clive assured me, his eyes connecting with mine without lifting his head. "You call the mantra as part of your daily ritual for forty days, and you will be taken care of. You know, I've tried so many times and I've never made it forty days." He chuckled, disbelief in his tone.

"What is the mantra?" I questioned.

"*Om Gam Ganapataye Namaha Sharanam Ganesha,*" Clive spoke without hesitation, the sounds forming like a beat upon a hand drum.

He repeated it again at half the speed. The sounds filled the entire space, each syllable echoing in my ears.

"Only thirty-nine more days to go," I replied, repeating the mantra in my mind again and again, forgetting the sounds as soon as I stopped.

His machine repeated the Ganesh's mantra over my hip, pushing each sound further into my skin.

Clive's hand was precise and bold. His lines were heavy and used sparingly. The drawing bounced off my skin and demanded your attention, the motion created by his arms and trunk drawing your eye back into the center of the piece, and out again to absorb the details.

He'd moved onto shading and then filling in the lines with color; the flesh of the creature a bold pink, patches of skin showing through underneath to create dimension on the elephant's surface. He cocked his head side to side as he lifted the machine from the skin to decide what to do next, where to move within the lines. There was occasional relief of my skin being wet down, wiped, then starting again. Hours had passed; I turned my body's position around the table for him to access a new section upon command. I closed my eyes patiently, stretching my arms overhead and extending my fingertips. He'd allowed for a few short breaks, but appeared deeply involved and I wanted to be a model client. I laid still.

"This tattoo will not be leaving you anytime soon," The Frenchy quipped. "He's in there."

"Everyone leaves you, Clive. It's just a matter of when," I replied. "I found out that I don't need anyone, and that it's not all that bad. But I will keep the Ganesh."

I'm not sure why I said that, feeling my cheeks flush with shame.

"I guess you're right." His head down, his wrist making small circles as he drilled color into my dermis and blood stippled the surface of my skin.

"I'm almost done here," Clive offered; this was his first mention of a timeline since I began the sitting. I'd lost track of time. "I'm just going to clean up a couple of lines."

My gaze passed over his face and neck, and I saw a glimmer of metal at the collar of his shirt. He had a tiny gold charm of the *cornicello* hanging from a short chain on his neck. *Cornicello*, meaning "tiny horn."

"You Italian?" I questioned him out of the blue, confused.

A smile spread over his mouth.

"On my mom's side, yeah. Why do you ask? The name 'The Frenchy' give it away?" he joked with a titter in his voice.

"The *cornicello*. A dead giveaway."

"Ah, a fellow immigrant," he teased. "While I'm old enough to know that all that church business I was brought up in, the beliefs, I quickly learned it's never been for me. But some habits die hard. I follow much more Eastern practices, now."

He pulled his gloves off and hooked his pointer finger into the neck of his shirt, pulling it down to reveal a tattoo of the evil eye which sat directly under the horn. The horn protected against dangers, along with the evil eye: a malevolent glare cast your way would follow you like a curse, so protection was needed. Nonna used to become ill and tell me that someone's gaze had cast a spell on her, believing it made her feel nauseous. She'd say the Hail Mary prayer repeatedly, raising the *cornicello* to her mouth to clear the curse. If that didn't work, she had a ceremony of sorts to perform.

"My Nonna had always been a firm believer in the evil eye!" my voice jumping an octave. "She would pour a small dish of holy water and set it on the table. Then, she'd take a pair of scissors and cut the air three times over the top of the dish." I looked at Clive, his face smiling and a slow nod of recognition in his gesture.

"She'd repeat her chant, or mantra, I guess, once in English and once in Italian."

> *Envy and the evil eye*
> *Keep your horns within your eyesight.*
> *Death to envy, and may the evil eye explode!*
> *In the name of God and Holy Mary*
> *May the evil eye go away!*
> *Holy Monday, Holy Tuesday, Holy*
> *Wednesday, Holy Thursday, Holy Friday,*
> *Holy Saturday,*
> *and to Easter Sunday, the evil eye dies!"*

A sharp laugh escaped from The Italian Frenchy's throat as I dramatically recited Nonna's prayer in a theatrical cadence.

"She'd pour some salt into the dish and make the sign of the cross three times. Then she'd cut the water and sign the water again."

Giggling, I remembered thinking she'd become a witch the first time I saw her perform this.

"She'd toss out the water and repeat this entire setup two more times!" We were both chuckling; our laughs trailed off.

"Nonna would be happy to know you were being tattooed by a believer," he teased. "Actually, Nonna would not be happy at all to know you were being tattooed! We'll keep it to ourselves."

He reached for the horn and raised it to his lips.

Giggles overtook us again until my side hurt. It felt so good, so unfamiliar to laugh freely. Guilt tried to creep in for enjoying this moment, but I held it down inside. I took the first full look at my leg and stopped. The Ganesh rested; complete, in his perfection.

"The Ganesh is the Indian equivalent to the *cornicello*, I suppose," Clive proposed. "There is no better way to protect yourself from evil, Catholic or otherwise."

With that comment, he turned his stool toward his station and reached for fresh gloves to begin his clean-up.

Pushing myself off the edge of the table, I walked up close to the mirror and took in the powerful statue. Each detail had been completely considered. I still had Dylan's Ganesh drawing rolled up in the tube on the floor by my bag, but this proved better. The outcome was more than he'd imagined; more than I'd imagined. Reaching for the tube, I unrolled the papers and freed his original drawing. I sifted through the drawings and grabbed the corner of the Ganesh I'd brought along with me.

I held up Dylan's drawing to the mirror, letting the remaining stencils fall in curls to the floor. Moving my arms away from my body and tilting the drawing about twenty degrees, Dylan's lines fell over top of The Frenchy's Ganesh. They were in near unison, the trunk on each elephant taking the same curved path. Dylan always followed the rules of drawing a tattoo very closely, and this moment was proof. The burning sensation over my hip and thigh began to intensify, and I pulled Dylan's drawing away from my leg.

Clive crouched to the floor at my pile of stencils and had pulled the Fudo Myo-o from the stack.

"Horiyoshi III," he stated, matter-of-fact.

"Crows and Herons," citing the book I'd pulled it from.

"A true master of this craft." He said, running his fingers along the strong strokes of the Fudo's shoulder in black ink.

"Where are these stencils from?" Clive questioned, gently, his hand gathering the remaining papers and respectfully reviewing each image. The kitsune, the heron, and Dylan's Ganesh.

"My, ah, my husband drew them."

As our eyes locked, tears welled up without warning.

"He's dead." I swallowed the mass gathered in my throat, but it didn't pass. I wanted to answer his question before he asked it, to save myself the embarrassment.

"He was quite the tattooer, I suspect," his eyes locked on Dylan's lines.

It hurt to hear these words, to know how Dylan would have given life to hear that from Clive The Frenchy.

"Tight, clean hand. Drew with intention. Played by the rules. I would have liked him." He sighed. "All the young guys are all about breaking the rules now. They don't outline, they don't use black shading, they don't even draw, it seems. They simply trace now. Your husband was truly passing on the trade, the way it's meant to be done. It's a shame he's gone, Annalise. For you, and for tattooing. I'm very sorry." His hand reached for me, clasped my wrist, and gave it a brief squeeze.

Tears streamed down my cheeks, and I didn't bother to try and hold back.

"Tattooing often takes more than it gives, I know."

His voice was soothing; he understood and let me sit in the moment safely. I was grateful for the private room. He pulled the Ganesh stencil gently from my fingers and turned to roll the papers back into the tube, giving me a moment of privacy.

I rubbed my fingertips deep into my eyes until I saw spots of light. My hip felt tender in the open air, and I looked to Clive to see him preparing bandages for me to be wrapped up. With each tattoo I collected, I began to understand the ritual. The ritual I'd seen hundreds of times over the years in pieces had now become ingrained in me, like a small creek working its way through rough land—the surface being carved in a pattern that my mind could memorize.

"Where will you head now?" he asked, as I examined the top of his head while he wrapped the surgical tape around my thigh, securing the blue bandaging in place.

I hadn't thought about it yet. I should have come to expect this question by now, but I still acted surprised each time it was presented to me. I'd never thought how to plan for what came next. *What would be the resolve?* I thought. With each tattoo, I'd begun to gain strength and life and color, but I felt empty, still afraid to disappoint Dylan.

"I'm not sure," I replied with honesty.

"You need to ride out to the University," his chin pointing to the wall, I assumed in the direction of the campus.

"Huh?" I grunted.

"The University of British Columbia," he stated.

"The campus has the most magical Japanese garden you've ever seen. Every bloom and blossom you'd find in a Japanese bodysuit will be in that place." The corners of his lips curling as he stood to meet my gaze.

"You're just in time to see the ginkgo trees in all their glory."

His hand fanned across the air between us, feeling for the leaves of the trees.

"They're bright yellow; the whole garden glows with them."

He pulled the black gloves from his hands and tossed them onto the blood-stained drop cloth on the bed.

"If you wait too long, the fruit on the tree begins to rot and the whole garden smells so foul you can't step near it!" He chuckled at the thought. "They say it smells like, well, vomit!" His hand reflexively reached for his stomach as if suddenly ill.

I pictured lush yellow trees filled with tiny mouths instead of leaves.

"That's quite the thought!" I retorted, excited to explore the gardens.

Dylan's fingers tightened around my throat at the thought; he'd drawn budding and blooming ginkgo trees and leaves in patterned symmetry many times before. The delicate leaves were each shaped like a fan, scaled for a porcelain doll.

"I read that it's Canada's oldest Botanical Garden. It's named after some Japanese scholar, Nitobe." His eyes flicked up, searching for the details in his memory. "I love taking my wife there; it's like a walk through history. There are plants, trees, and water. I read on the sign that the garden is organized like time; one section is a day, another is a week, and another is a year! I'm not a gardener or anything, but I can appreciate that place." He shook his head, looking down to the ground. "Anyway, I hope you can make it there."

With that, he began moving to the door, and I knew this was my cue.

My time with The Frenchy had ended.

CHAPTER 36

"What'll it be?" I looked up to meet eyes with a man about my age behind the counter. I found myself sitting at the bar of a long, narrow restaurant in Chinatown.

"Beer, please," nodding my chin toward the taps. "Surprise me."

My heels were hitched onto the support bar on the bottom of the stool, and my helmet rested on the counter next to me. I'd adjusted to spending so much time alone that I found myself avoiding interactions with the bartender and keeping to myself. The bar's top was crafted of copper, and the patina it had acquired was like looking into the bottom of a pond; the history of previous customers and staff left behind in fingerprints and drink stains. The deep fryer's scent filled the air, and every seat aside from one had filled in the place. Friends sat close together, leaning in, laughter filling the conversations. The Ganesh burned hot under my jeans, and the tape holding the bandaging in place sat pulling at my skin, causing tiny spikes of pain as I shifted on the stool.

Scrolling through my phone, I searched for directions to the University grounds. I'd go in the morning to take a look at the yellow blooming trees and test their scent. *How did I end up here?* I wondered to myself, looking around the room.

I thought of my mother back home. Having left so suddenly, I knew she was worried if I was safe, but I couldn't bring myself to reach out and tell her what I had been doing, where I had been, or where I would head next. Guilt flushed my cheeks, and my stomach felt hollow. I had acted with selfishness, an unfamiliar state in which to be.

"Mom," the contact read in my phone. My thumb hovered over the phone icon as I hesitated, quickly touching the button and raising the device to my ear with a shaking hand. As it rang, my whole body washed with fear; I hadn't had to explain myself in weeks.

"Annalise!" my mother exclaimed, happiness in her voice. "Where are you? Are you safe?" A long pause filled the line.

"Mom. Hi," I replied, the fear subsiding and a smile spreading across my lips. "I'm safe. I'm very well actually, Mom, honestly." I waited for her to reply.

"Where are you?" she asked again with a gentle tone.

She wasn't upset, and the worry in her voice had tempered.

"It's a long story, but I'm on the road, clearing my head." A vague reply, not sure why I didn't want to share the details.

"Mom, I'm sorry," a lump of emotion forming in my throat.

"There's nothing to be sorry for, Honey. There is no script for what you're dealing with. If you're safe and you're healing, then that's all I can ask for."

A comfortable silence took hold for a few moments. I could hear her light breathing into the phone, a familiar sound.

"I think I have one more stop I need to make before I can come back, Mom."

The realization of my last destination was coming fully into view.

"I will be a while yet," my tone was firm, but quiet.

"Okay, do you need anything, Annalise?" She wanted to help, but she'd helped enough.

"You know, I'm actually okay, Mom." I believed it when I said that.

"I can see again. I can hear again."

I'm not sure what I intended by that statement, but I knew she understood.

"I will call you before I come back, I promise. Don't worry about me."

I pushed my finger into my other ear blocking out the friendly conversation in the restaurant.

"Okay, Annalise. We love you."

I ended the call and covered my phone with both hands. The real world was still waiting for me out there, and I knew I could go back to it safely—but not yet.

CHAPTER 37

$\mathscr{T}$he next morning, my bike waited packed by 8:00 a.m., and I was ready to navigate my way out to the University's grounds, following the ocean as best I could for the ride. The Pacific's waters were powerful this morning, and the streets were littered with pedestrians walking their commutes with coffees in hand. Vancouver looked like a drawing; the people all fit, the plants were manicured, and the buildings all glistened with an aqua glow cast by the sun and water.

The ride out to the botanical garden took me about thirty minutes; I rolled in as the students began marching the pathways for the day. Leaving my helmet with my bike, I had Dylan's jacket tucked under my arm, my backpack hanging from my shoulders, and the drawing tube wedged tightly in tow. I had settled into my outfit, no longer feeling like others were looking at me as if I were wearing a costume. The Lord of Beginnings wrapped around my body tightly on one side, the kitsune shifting my powers on the other. They forced me forward, holding me up and planting my feet to the earth with each step.

My deities and I arrived at our destination. The walk had led to the entrance of the gardens; a modest wooden placard welcomed us to the well-tended grove. The lush alcove led me into the gardens with tangled and detailed leaves hanging overhead. I stopped and grabbed a perfectly formed leaf between my fingers, examining it as it pointed toward me. Its saturated surface bright with chlorophyll and veined in yellow streams, all running to the central lifeline of the branch.

Releasing the leaf, the branch snapped back into its place. Thankfully, signage and tidy plaques detailing my journey took me on a walking tour of what lies ahead. My eyes scanned the grounds before me; strict placements and organization struck me in contrast to the flow of the plants, greenery, and textured earth. Two lanterns caught my attention, my mind darting back to a book on Dylan's shelf. Lanterns were a Chinese invention brought to Japan. They first lighted doorways to shrines and temples and then were made of stone and placed in Japanese gardens as part of the tea ceremony. Warmth filled my fingertips as I applied this reading to the world in front of me. I found myself in a shrine, a sacred capsule of Japan brought to North America in the heart of Inazō Nitobe. My gaze clung to a statue just ahead.

Nitobe stood proud in bust form, cast in bronze. Following the intended path, I arrived before him and examined his face, soft and welcoming despite being set in metal. The balls of his cheeks shone where visitors had rubbed them smooth. Black pitting had formed on his shoulders, and streaks of rain bore pathways down his chest. He stared just past me. I stood on my tip-toes trying to reach his line of sight, but his eye-line fell above me, looking over the entry to the grounds.

His placard read, "*Dr. Inazō Nitobe (1862-1933) was an agriculturalist, scholar, Quaker, philosopher, statesman, and educator. Dr. Nitobe was educated at Sapporo Agricultural College, University of Tokyo, Johns Hopkins, and the University of Halle in Germany. Early in his life, he expressed the desire to be a 'bridge over the Pacific' and he devoted much of his life to promoting trust and understanding between North America and Japan.*"

My fingers skipped lightly over the letters of this sign. I ran them back and forth over the same line, "*bridge over the Pacific,*" until they were devoid of sense. I raised my hands to my lips and slowly touched my fingers to my tongue; they tasted of metal and dirt and gasoline. Closing my eyes, I pictured Nonna and Nonno's graves, imagining them each cast in bronze, their sculpted torsos floating above their buried bodies like beacons.

The sunlight danced on the back of my eyelids with strobing, colored patterns. I opened my eyes to small slits and let the greenery creep back in. My feet were drawn to a low grassy mound where I could get the best view of the entire garden. It felt like I was floating over the lush and well-loved grass; stopping abruptly, I knelt to the ground. Feeling the denim tighten and pinch around my new tattoo, I winced slightly as I reached for my boots.

Working quickly, I unlaced my boots, hooked my fingers into the back of my socks, and pulled them off my feet, stuffing them into the boots. Tying the laces together in a loose knot, I slung them through my backpack strap and felt them bounce off my hip on occasion. The grass felt cool and firm in my toes; I spread them wide and let the blades work in between each digit. I balanced on the balls of my feet and stretched my hands overhead, feeling the pull of the earth and the freedom of the sky at the same time.

From the knoll, I could see each bridge connecting the sections of the gardens; I counted six. *The bridge over the Pacific.* Drawn to a particular bridge, I started to make my way toward it, digging my feet into the earth with each step. The entrance of the bridge held a small sign that read "*ZigZag Bridge*" near the iris pond. The words on the bottom of the sign read "*Devil-Losing Bridge.*" I knew about zig-zag bridges, as Dylan had drawn many of them over the years. He always placed them at the bottom of the drawing, inviting your eye to climb up the page. Below the bridge, he'd draw demons and spirits melting and burning in a fire, and above the bridge, trees, cherry blossoms, flowers, and brightly colored birds. The drawings were a look into his mind; below the bridge, the parts of Dylan that he held down the best he could, and across the zig-zag bridge: the freedom his mind searched for.

He explained to me that there is a belief in Japan that evil spirits can only travel in straight lines, so if you cross this bridge in its zig-zag pattern, the spirits cannot follow you and you will be free. My heart tightened, and I repeated the words again in my mind. *The spirits cannot follow you and you will be free.*

Steadying my hands on each side of the bridge's railings, I reached my foot out toward the first plank and pressed down. My bare toe could feel the moisture from the ocean that had absorbed into the wood. I dragged my toe back toward myself and felt the ridges in the wood as my foot skipped over the board. Leaning forward, I balanced my weight all onto one foot. I wanted to run across the bridge, but my body tingled full of hesitation; the evil spirits were steps away from being left behind, and I knew what that meant. That meant that Dylan would leave me; he would be gone.

"Dylan," my voice cracked.

Tears filled my eyes, my throat full of pressure and tension and pain.

"I'm going to leave you now," I confessed to him.

"I loved you, you know?"

I stepped onto the bridge, tears spilling down my cheeks.

Each step felt cold and sharp under my feet; I moved slowly along the zig-zagged boards, dragging my fingertips along the railings. My eyes focused on the bright yellow blossoms of the ginkgo trees ahead. I drew a long stream of air in through my nose, wondering if I'd made it to the trees in time. The oxygen felt fresh, clean, and bright. Reaching the end of the bridge, I looked to my feet, waiting at the last board. Tears blurred my eyes, and my throat filled with pressure. I hopped off the bridge onto the grass with two feet landing at once. Dropping to my knees, I felt the moisture of the grass seeping through my jeans. I ran my hands over my thighs, over the kitsune, over the Ganesh, over Dylan's drawings, over my life.

The feeling of fear is impossible to describe accurately, I thought to myself. *Is that what this feeling is? This tension pulling my limbs to the grass?* Fear is to feel hesitation in every waking and sleeping moment of your existence as it tells you that you can't. To feel crippled by choice, by time, by others, by yourself. To feel judgment and loss and longing and want. Fear is the color of your own eyes in the mirror, and fear is the voices and sounds that fill your brain even when you're begging to turn them off. Fear is not simple or kind or delicate. It is as sharp as a sword whose only aim is to pierce your heart and watch it drain you of blood. Fear pulses in your fingertips and echoes in your ears. Fear does not sleep, it does not forgive, and it cannot listen. It surrounds your body like a bush of barbed thorns, begging you to take a step.

I tilted my face to the grass and let the tears run freely off my cheeks into the blades below me—returned to the ground. My arms and legs felt cast in bronze like the statue of Nitobe. I willed them to move.

"This is fear, this is the feeling right here, and it's not real, Annalise," I whispered to myself, a low sob escaping my lips. "It's not real."

Raising my shoulders up, I pushed out my chest. Latching my fingers into the collar of my sweater, I pulled down the neck and gazed down at the tiny crow's skull being carried away by the heron. I stretched my arms to my sides and flexed the wings of the heron; the wind swept me up by my feathers, and it carried me up to the tree as the air rushed over my face. Gazing down at the gardens, geometric patterns and colors danced on the ground below, gathered in a ring by the yellow ginkgos. The heron lifted me higher, and I could see only shapes like the first reliefs into a woodcut print block before the image had taken form. I held the space over the gardens, casting a shadow across every inch, turning the bright morning into night, but the darkness appeared only temporarily. I knew the darkness to simply be fear. I was not afraid of this flight; I could float here forever.

Opening my eyes, I stared into the bright yellow center of the ginkgo tree before me. It became a solar eclipse and filled the sky, edge to edge with its life-giving glow. The tree had an answer for me; it waited right there. I'd read about it many times, and it became very clear to me why I had been brought here. The yellow foliage offered an object of veneration, symbolizing the unity of opposites.

"The ginkgo is a symbol of changelessness. Why would you ever want that tattooed?" I remember Dylan stating, to no one, as he prepared a drawing for a client's piece.

I'd researched it the next day at work; it was a misunderstood ideogram. He'd clung to the negative. The book of *Japanese Gardens* read, *"The ginkgo possesses miraculous powers; it is the marker of hope and of unmeasured pasts. It is a symbol of love."* My fingertip sat on the word love.

CHAPTER 38

How did I end up here? I wondered, thinking about where I'd been in the last few months, questioning if I still had a place back home. The further away I got from my life, the less familiar everything felt.

My nostrils flared in refute as the odor assaulted my senses. My throat flexed, trying to force the smell out of my cavities. I squinted my eyes shut tightly, afraid the smell would enter through the moist cells of my eyes. The Frenchy had been right; it smelled just like vomit. I wondered if they smelled the same in Vancouver as it did here. Did the distance and air and surroundings change the experience? I could not say.

Crossing the ocean, autumn followed me east. The female ginkgo trees' fruit began to rot just in time for my arrival to Japan; it produced an acrid and pungent smell that discouraged visitors from getting too close. I stood next to the base of the trees, turning my head side to side, watching the dioecious foliage line the walkway before me in either direction. Nothing looked familiar here.

These ginkgo trees were older, the bases thicker, and the roots rougher along the surface of the ground. The ginkgos I'd seen in Vancouver were leaner, lighter, more youthful. The ginkgos in Japan were solid, thick, and deeply entrenched. I crouched down to touch a rotting berry, the smell of rancid butter left on my fingertips. As I rose, I came shoulder to shoulder with a slight man dressed in a lightly quilted coat and holding an umbrella, despite the sky being dry. He wore a paper mask over his nose and mouth, but his sensing eyes smiled at me.

I nodded my head, *"Kon'nichiwa,"* I whispered, not confident in my pronunciation.

"Hello," he replied.

Relief took over my chest, realizing he spoke English.

He lifted his hand to his mask, the skin delicate and creamy on the back of his fingers with a few dark hairs twisted on each knuckle. He tugged the mask down and hitched it below his chin, pinching his nose in drama like a silent film. I smiled and laughed lightly, nodding in agreement.

"The ginkgo lady tree is very naughty this time of year," he offered, wagging his finger at the bark. "But so many miss out on all of the beauty just because of the smell."

He turned to me, our eyes connecting.

"My grandmother, *soba*, she told me that the lady ginkgo is the strongest tree in the universe."

I could feel the wind licking the hem of my dress, allowing the kitsune's tails to feel the fresh October air. I held the seam in place at my knee, ensuring that the ink would not be visible.

"The trees are so strong, so powerful, that they have been here since the dinosaur's time. They gave shade and food and love." His voice came out low, dotted like a metronome.

His accent was very light; I wondered if he'd traveled the world and returned to this spot years later.

"I do not know if we planted these trees near the temples or if the temples were built near the trees, but the ginkgos guard our fane for centuries." He looked away from the treeline, sucking in a deep breath of the decomposing berries.

I stared at the tree trunk in its naturalized land—sturdy and ancient. Its roots bound deeply into the ground, its ability to survive unmatched.

"There were many years that *soba* said that the ginkgo was gone from this place." He waved his hand near the ground, erasing the trees from their pits. "But no! Six perfect ginkgos stood strong, surviving Hiroshima's blast." His eyes widened, and he nodded slowly at me, ensuring I understood. "Those same trees are still standing there, in Hiroshima," he told me.

He stomped each foot hard into the ground. I gazed at his small feet, barely showing from the hem of his dark brown trousers. Wisps of dust still swirling around his toes from the movement.

"*Soba* told me, once the food and the shelter for the dinosaurs, now growing from the soil where their bones are buried, feeding the trees instead." A smirk raised the corners of his mouth, his eyes closed for an extra moment, likely thinking of his grandmother.

He reached for my hand slowly and pulled me toward the trunk, placing my palm onto the rough, dry surface.

"This is a fossil. This tree is a time capsule."

He placed his hand over the back of mine and pulled it gently down the trunk, my fingers skipping lightly over its texture.

"Two-hundred-seventy million years, that is how old these trees are."

I looked up, watching the tiny umber fans move in unison across the sky, picturing them casting shadows over the Jurassic era.

"How do you know that?" I questioned.

Unsure of the age of the universe altogether, I was suddenly unsure of the soil I stood on and the man I was speaking to. *How could anyone know that?* I doubted.

"I believe the stories in the temples, dear," he replied, with calm patience. "The ginkgo leaf is carved into the statues, and they guard the entrances; they shade the homes and feed the workers. They decorate the cloth and are pressed into the rocks and soil."

His statement was offered very matter-of-fact. "You don't see them unless you look," his voice steady. "Why have you traveled here?" he asked.

"I didn't have a choice," I replied.

"We always have a choice," he said. "You can choose to evolve, or you can choose to repeat." His arms still at his sides.

"What if I don't evolve?" I asked, worry knit through my brow.

"You become stuck to the ground like the ginkgo tree." His voice traveled so softly.

"Unmeasured pasts," I replied.

"You know, people think change is the hardest action to accomplish. But it's not, really. You can change very quickly if you can stop holding on so tightly." His hands gathered in front of his chest, squeezing the air tightly.

"What if all you can do is survive?" I asked. "Not evolve, not repeat, just survive?" I searched his face for an answer.

"You have done much more than survive, I would guess." His eyes were very soft and watery in their gaze.

"I ran away," I confessed.

"You can always go back; Just leave behind the parts that you cannot carry anymore before you do," He replied. "Or, you can gather what you need and then go back. Sometimes, it's not always about taking away; sometimes it's about collecting. We all do what we must to protect our hearts, our minds, our stability," he glanced to the tree before us, "there is no shame in choosing yourself."

With that, he pulled the paper mask back over his nose and lips. He reached the tree branch that bent toward him, plucking a single yellow leaf by its thin stem. He twirled it between his fingers, back and forth quickly until it became a three-dimensional shape. With a bob of his head, he carried on past me. His figure followed the line of trees along the walkway framing the port's edge in the park.

CHAPTER 39

*T*he streets of Yokohama were much plainer than I'd imagined, especially after traveling to the city through Tokyo, where all of your senses were constantly engaged. The buildings were low and grey, modest and dingy.

The city wove its way around the water's edge; tourists crowded the pathways leading to a busy Ferris wheel and a permanently static ship marking this city's historical evolution in the Minatomirai center. An intense crowd of locals and tourists was concentrated at the mouth of the Yamashita Park that led through Minotomirai and up to the edge of the ocean.

As I followed the boardwalk toward the park, I noticed gateways of roses framing the head of a few distinct footpaths. The roses were grand and loved in a way that I could feel. Each vine was guided up a trellis; each petal proudly faced the sun. I'd never seen anything quite like the rows of trellises that welcomed me. As I stepped closer, I noticed they were entrances to a spectacular rose garden full of colors and shapes and varieties beyond my imagination.

There were rectangular beds uniformly laid out in a grid before me, with people dotting the pathways. Each bed contained a different variation of the classic flower. There were purples, lavenders, pinks, crisp whites, bright corals, and deep burgundies organized before me. Stepping onto the pathways, I could see small towers of roses, guided up like columns. Bright red, butter yellow, and periwinkle blues marked the corners of the pathways and guided me through the gardens. Crouching down, I balanced at the edge of a bed of bright orange roses. The shape of the petals came to sharp points; they were unlike any rose I'd ever come across.

My mind shot to Dylan's drawings; roses were one of his favorite subject matters to draw. He'd often create the images for flash sheets, pre-drawn sets of designs with a common theme. In the center of one of his rose flash sheets was a perfectly drawn rose with pointed petals. I always thought this had just been a stylized rendering, but here I sat, in front of this exact flower. Instead of the center of the flower darkening, it faded to a light peach hue and disappeared into the pistils in the middle. Framed by rich green leaves, there was perfection in their placement and shiny contrasting coats.

Reaching for a petal, I acted carefully to not damage the flower. The petal felt like silk between my fingers as I rubbed it. The fragrant perfume of the flowers danced under my nostrils, cleansing away any remainder of ginkgo berries. It suddenly dawned on me why the rows of ginkgo trees were framed with such an abundance of perfumed blossoms. They were working as yin and yang for the people carefully passing through.

Tipping forward onto my knees, I rested my weight onto my heels. Looking down the pathways, I watched the small groups of people moving through the gardens. The Japanese were very slight in stature, narrow in the hips and shoulders. The women dressed with extreme elegance and modesty; long skirts flowed to the ankles, sleeves down to the wrists, delicate jewelry, and simple hairstyles. Many carried umbrellas to protect their untouched skin from the sun, and many had gloved hands. There were likely one hundred people wandering the gardens, yet the air hung nearly silent. Quiet observation and consideration in public spaces was a common tradition here in Japan, but so uncommon at home; modesty was not part of our culture anymore. I suddenly felt naked in my short dress, tugging the hem of it to cover my knees as best I could in this position.

A few of the patrons wore paper masks covering the nose and mouth portions of their faces. Just dark eyes framed with dark hair peered down at the roses. A group of young schoolgirls, all in perfectly matching uniforms, were chattering and giggling, providing the only punctuation of sound in the vast space.

I stared deep into the center of a perfectly formed yellow rose. Dylan had a yellow rose tattooed on the back of his left hand. "A job-stopper," he chuckled when he pulled back the bandage and showed it to me. The back of the hand looked tough and worked and touched by the sun; it showed every pore and hair follicle when I studied the black lines forming the petals disappearing in the center. His veins lightly rippled below the surface; he clenched his palms into a fist, and the rose flexed and stretched to a taught and clear position.

The golden and amber rose expressed hope, promise, and new beginnings, surrounded by the contrasting thorns. The few thorns that poked out around the edges of his hand stood for loss, defense, and thoughtlessness. He looked up at me, studying his hand, and said, "yellow roses symbolize a mature love." Those words created a pit in my stomach. A mature love that I had been stuck in, my feet embedded into the ground with the thorny vines tangled between each toe; dare I take a step, I'd bleed.

CHAPTER 40

*M*oving through the city, I felt like a guest. I touched my feet lightly to the ground with each step, trying to go unnoticed by those around me, though no one took observation of the space I occupied. The cityscape broke out into many small neighborhoods as I wandered, each with its own distinct markers. The roadway opened into a community with a repeat of shops lining each side. I glanced through the glass window on my left and watched two women sitting in front of mirrors having their hair styled, a daily ritual underway.

I walked until my toes ached in the ends of my boots. I examined the signage pinned to the fronts of the buildings as I turned down a narrow side street, the sidewalk unforgiving below me. I stopped and rested against the wall; a paper sign written in English was crudely taped to the inside of the glass window next to me. Leaning forward, I read the typed print, "*This area is often patrolled by police.*" This caught me off guard; the area looked safe and clean and did not seem to require a police presence.

Raising my hand over my brows to block the sun, I pressed my face to the glass. My gaze fixed back and forth, looking first through the glass and then back to my reflection in the window.

There were two mats on the ground, each made of a fibrous weave and covered with finely patterned cushions. Skinny bookshelves lined the walls I could see from the street, books stacked into every corner, spines facing both directions; the stacks created small, self-contained units, each resembling an aging apartment complex on a cliff's edge.

The Easel jumped to mind; the smell filled my nostrils from memory, and I felt safe on this street. I stepped sideways toward the door and reached for the handle; a golden bell hung from the knob with a red, silky tassel dangling from its end. It gave a clunky jingle as I pulled the door open and stepped inside. A young woman glanced up at me, and I nodded deeply toward her, my torso bowing. She held my stare and gave a slight nod in return. Crouching slowly, I pulled my boots off my feet and tucked them neatly under the bench by the door. Placing my backpack quietly on the hook nearby, she gestured for me to enter.

A shielded place, but I was welcome here. My hands rose to my chest, and I placed my flattened palms over the heron's wings, gliding my fingers out toward my shoulders. She looked to be a heron, too. I could tell.

"*Kon'nichiwa,*" I whispered, nodding again.

"Ah, *Kon'nichiwa*!" she mouthed back, pleased I had attempted to pronounce the greeting in Japanese. "Come, come. We invite you in." She raised her gloved hand and pulled me over to her with a gesture.

Her English came out perfectly, but not confident; the cadence of her tone was light and as thin as spring ice on a pond.

She knelt on a mat, her toes flexed onto the hard wooden floor, her knees sitting tightly bent on a cushion, and her bottom hovering above her heels. She leaned over her client—her subject—her canvas.

A young woman was lying before her on top of the dark-colored cushions. She waited, positioned on her front, laid out flat on her stomach. She appeared naked, aside from a small cloth rolled into a thong, providing her modesty in this private moment. My eyes darted to her head, to her toes, and scanned the designs all over her body. Her black hair was a rich blanket fanned out around her, providing a protective screen. Her small, rounded feet were sitting gently at the foot of the mat, covered in light pink slippers.

I steadily stepped closer and lowered myself beside her. The women welcomed me without speaking and allowed me to join them. Perching myself on a square cushion in a kneeling position, I placed my palms flat on my thighs. Shallow breaths entered my body through my nose, and I became aware of the space that I occupied in their ritual. My body became lighter than the air, and I felt myself hovering over the mat, the heron spreading her wings and protecting this moment from the sun.

In the center of her back, there lived a large skull with a thick and writhing snake woven through its eye-socket and mouth. Surrounding the centerpiece, capping the shoulder and cupping the hip, were lotus flowers, some were colored in blue, while the rest were red. My eyes were pulled down the body with the flow of the drawing, getting lost in the curves of black waves and water that crested her bottom and capped off the backs of her thighs just above the bend of the knee.

The bodysuit, or *irezumi,* appeared bold, heavy, and intimidating, but spiritual, light, and welcoming at the same time. There were stipples of blood in the waves where the needles had been entering her skin for the past few hours, but this time, the ritual had been different. The color was being forced in by hand, using a long wooden stick with needles secured at the end, the *nomi.*

I watched with anticipation, waiting for the needles to enter the skin being forced in by hand without the assistance of an electrically charged machine. *Tebori* meant hand carving, the original technique of tattooing, the customary method here before me. She took her hand and spread the skin tight on the fleshy thigh, and angled the stick down towards the skin. The tip of the needles all entered at once, creating a tiny satisfying burst as the skin gave way to the metal and ink. Her fingers moved with instinct, reflexes guiding the black wash over the patch of skin to create the full pattern desired. A slow process unfolded, bowing to traditionalism and respecting the process of this task. She used a thrust motion like a lever, called *tsuki-bori*, and a push-and-pull motion that seemed feathery, called *hanebori.*

Searching for her bare flesh, I landed on her creamy arms, comparing where she'd started her adornment as she laid out before her master. The attachment to her culture ran deep, so deep that she'd disrobe and offer her being to a fellow woman with trust and time and patience and pain.

The Japanese versions of skulls in tattooing were not demonized like the Western symbols we've become accustomed to. Rather, they celebrated life and death, change, and the possibility of what came after your soul left your body.

This thought got stuck in my mind. *Was my soul still with my body, or did Dylan take it with him?* I thought. I opened my mouth into a wide oval and sucked as much air in as I could. Suddenly, I realized I didn't want him to keep my soul; I needed it still, I deserved it still.

Staring down into the skull, I followed the lines of the snake around her faint muscles. The snake's significance often had also been misunderstood. The snake wrapped around her tightly, joining with the skull and providing protection from illness of the body and illness of the mind; it warded off misfortune and brought the carrier wisdom. Luck. Strength. And most significantly, the power to change.

How would she know if she'd really changed? I thought. *Would she feel different once these markings were on her back?* I pictured her in her old age, her cloak of protection weathered, worn, and unrecognizable. *Her hours of pain and patience rewarded with what?* The person who commits to a tattoo such as this on the scale of a bodysuit, in the manner of traditional *tebori,* possessed the exact balance of forbearance and impulse.

The lotus flowers capped off the edges of the designs, decorating her slight frame with bold blues and reds. The lotus flower carried many ideograms in Japan, each defined by color. The blue lotus marked mind over matter, bringing spirituality to win over compulsion. The red lotuses were Dylan's favorites. They were the heart lotus. They stood for the state of the heart; they brought love, understanding, and passion, and represented idealism in love.

What demons did this young, creamy-skinned woman carry deep within the chambers of her own heart? What lives had she endured to need this cape? The *nomi* moved in and out of her flesh; no one spoke a word. My fingers slowly guided up to her head a short distance across the floor and reached for her black, silky mane. I gently touched the tips of her hair, sure not to disturb her. It felt coarser than I'd expected, thick and firm under the pressure of my fingers.

Tattooing this way started in Japan in the Edo period, the 1600s. The method had begun as carving into wood blocks for prints, dipping them into ink and pressing them onto the surface of paper. The job title for both tattooers and woodcarvers were titled the same, *horishi*.

They shared imagery and celebrated art in a cultural lexicon that would be appropriated by the world. The sign on the window suddenly made sense. Even though Japan had been the origin of this craft for the East, it remained illegal in the country. Dylan had told me you needed to be a licensed doctor in the country to provide the services. I remember laughing at this thought of tattooers being doctors. It seemed absurd.

My eyes darted around the walls, noticing the village scenes pressed from carved board to paper, hanging like scrolls. I studied the miniature, uniform figures filling the streets and sidewalks like plastic toys. Waves curled around the edges of the print and the sky had been comprised of fine markings, laid methodically by the artist's hands. How many lines were in this print? Staring at the top left corner, I scanned across the printed paper and noticed each shape, the curl of the gouging tool, the pressure of the artist's fingers. *Nishiki-e*. I knew the word for this type of printing;

Dylan had many books on the subject, and proudly hung a samurai warrior *nishiki-e* on the wall of the shop, not far from where the bat lived.

This image hung so common, so ordinary; it was not religious, nor colonial. It did not feel important. There were no faces, no heroes, and no obvious protagonist. I could have been one of the figures in this print, my back turned to the watcher going on about my day on the streets, frozen in time in solid blue ink. There was a satisfying feeling viewing the secular; this was not a tale—but rather, reality. The people in the image wore long-sleeved shirts, long pants, long skirts. I wondered if their bodies were tattooed, cloaked in pattern and color and dreams.

The smoothed-skin client began to stir; I could see her discomfort in holding her still position for too long. The women began to speak in a near whisper, exchanging short sentences without looking at one another. Stepping up from the cushion I knelt on, I walked away from the women by slowly backing up, bowing my head in thanks. They needed their privacy to continue.

"*Arigatou gozaimasu,*" I said, repeating it again as I backed toward the door.

The craftswoman looked up and held my gaze. Smiling only with the corners of her mouth, she nodded her head in a deep bow. Her gloved fingers paused the needle as I exited the building.

CHAPTER 41

*P*eople filled the streets; the city appeared lower and less kept than the others I'd been to since arriving in Japan. I began following the flow of pedestrians as they were funneling over to Chinatown. Yokohama had the largest Chinatown in the country; twenty-one million visitors made the march each year to wander the streets jammed with vendors, food, shops, and the authentic aromas and exotic atmosphere nestled into the city.

Chinatown in Yokohama sprung up when the city's port became open to foreign trade. I'd read the brief details on a placard in the train station when I'd arrived. Decorative archways were positioned in the cardinal directions following the traditional Chinese feng-shui geomancy. I looked up as I began to approach a powerful and ornate entrance. Strong, red columns anchored each side with three small rooftops ostentatious with texture, gold, tiles, and symbols I could not read. Chinese dragons were embossed into the frames, surrounded by geometric patterns reflecting the sun.

Looking down the street crowded with vendors and shops on each side, the bold red signs jumped out at my eyes. Lanterns were strung in gold and hung still in the early afternoon air. The corridor presented like a sacred hallway, generations of resilience, determination, and courage lining the rows.

Stepping through the street, I followed a small-statured couple with dark hair. My eyes rested on a fan sitting neatly in a window display; it was bright gold and shaped like a ginkgo leaf. I reached for the glass on the window and traced the shape of the fan with my fingertip, my skin skipping across the warm pane.

Tucking my hands behind my back, I linked my fingers together underneath my backpack; my knuckles brushed on the cardboard tube of Dylan's drawings as I toured through the century's worth of history, faces, and offerings.

Waiting in line outside of a restaurant that only served dumplings, I watched the cooks feverishly prepare the small bundles. Patterned in their symmetry, with doughs colored both pale green and cream.

Steam rose all around them as they worked to scale, preparing hundreds of morsels for the patiently waiting crowd. While watching the production line through the glass, my body began to feel anxious. I found myself stalling, spending time touring the area to avoid what I'd traveled to Yokohama to do. Shifting the weight between my feet, I reached behind me to feel the drawings secured onto my backpack. I had been stalling in this lineup, avoiding the destination I'd traveled across the world to arrive at. My stomach felt nervous, and dampness crept to my armpits as I looked around; my mind felt so full and overwhelmed being here on this street, alone.

Empirical fact is what my mind longed for, but the meaning of life is what my heart wanted to know. I'd never stopped to think if I deserved this path; *had Dylan happened to me, or did I create him?* I thought. His existence had etched a neural pathway in my brain, and the circuit still ran with such electricity it felt like a power surge jolting through my body, as if I'd touched my tongue to a light socket. I wanted to dull the feeling of him and take away his ability to live in my brain, but I had become terrified of being rewired and forgetting any moment that he'd created within me.

Is it possible to be concerned with the fate of the universe, the fate of my mind and body, and the fate of Dylan's soul all equally? I wondered. I'd been pulled through life by a magnet that he'd attached to me from beyond the passage of death. I dug my heels into the sidewalk as this idea captured my limbs, but there lived nothing on the other side. I felt certain of this. Death is without sensation. It dissolves us into nothing. It is devoid of pleasure and lost of conversation. It's not virtuous; it lacks desire, and it can digest your hurt without flinching. Dylan was death.

I no longer needed a worthy purpose to be here—here on this street, in Japan, on this planet, or in this universe. Looking down at my hand, I traced the letter "*A*" on my skin where Dylan had my initial tattooed. I needed to cross through the *torii* in my head, into the other side of this. A torii was a simple but sturdy gate that marked the entrance of the consecrated spaces across Japan.

Wandering the streets, I became numb to the toriis and temples scattered throughout the daily lives and businesses of the country. Four posts were placed in the sacred areas, and they were tethered together by rope. Connected by the woven cord holding strong, yet so easy to cross over. The rope showed me the outside versus the inside—the ordinary versus the holy. You could cross this threshold at will; you only had to accept it with your mind.

Standing at the window to the dumpling shop, a nearly translucent white bird fluttered to a gentle stop near the corner.

"Birds bring the dead in Japan," Dylan had quipped.

I rubbed my hand across my breast bone, checking on my heron silently, now fully healed and well-settled into the skin.

"You can become a white bird, and you can soar above everyone in your life, circling and circling, and you can select where you'd want to be buried."

I thought very little of his words when he'd said this to me, sitting at the kitchen table in our cold and creaky house. He constantly spoke of Japanese lore; these details didn't always stay with me.

"A bird can take on your dead soul, I believe."

Dylan's voice rang in my ears as I stared down at this bird, mindlessly pecking at the ground. I slid my toe out toward it and stomped my foot, forcing it to fly off with a start. Birds weren't welcome to cross the torii. I wanted to cross alone, anyway.

CHAPTER 42

*W*alking swiftly through the Nishi Ward, the buildings remained short and plain; I could have been anywhere. The detail and tradition that decorated every corner of Japan so far felt lost in this area of Yokohama. This ward looked functional and did not display any frills or colors or gimmicks. My chest pounded as I neared Hiranuma Street; my feet were floating across the sidewalk without effort. *How could I be heading here without Dylan?* I thought. *What would I say when I arrived?* Fear prickled my arms, and the fine hairs stood on end. I wiggled my fingers as if warming up to play a piano concert; they were tingling and numb.

The Hiranuma Street sign came into view as I approached the next block with my heart pounding in my ears. My backpack bounced off my hips, creating a quiet rhythm which my feet followed along to. Arriving at the corner, I turned left and a collage of small colors caught my attention. I knew I'd arrived; the ground-level window that I'd been searching for filled my view.

Tattooers from all over the world traveled to this window to add their shop's sticker to the glass canvas. I'd seen pictures of this window many times, and now I stood in front of it, reading all the shop names. Some were shaped like bumper stickers, and others were ovals and circles. The edges of the shapes touched and blocked out the glass. Many of the stickers had faded with the sun, reds turning to light pinks, dirt collecting around their borders. A narrow placard hung above the windows off-center; in modest capital letters, it read *TATTOO MUSEUM*. It looked more like an office building than a museum or tattoo shop, I thought. A teal-green sign hung next to the text bearing a shape that looked like a sword and a cup carefully balanced. A small number of Japanese characters that I could not read were brushed on in ink in the corner of the sign.

Walking through the front door, I turned into the congested space as the smell of cigarettes burned my nose. An older woman sat behind a crowded desk shrouded with paraphernalia and trinkets; she had to be in her seventies, a cigarette perched gently in her fingers. I knew from books that this had to be Horiyoshi's wife, Mayumi Nakano. She wore a fitted black t-shirt, deeply settled tattoos adorning each arm. A long necklace hung around her neck and her hair streaked with grey framed her face. She pointed to the yellowed paper sign taped to the desk. I paid the entry fee of 1000 Yen, and in turn, was given an enamel pin shaped like the cup and sword symbol which hung outside.

Squeezing the pin in its miniature plastic wrapping in the palm of my hand, I let the dull point dig into my skin. She nodded, permitting me to enter the curated maze and wander around.

The museum appeared tight and crooked and was packed from floor to ceiling. A slanted set of stairs led to the second floor, and angled beams and lines were at each turn. A glass case that lined a wall was filled with curious tattoo machines, hand-written tags next to each denoting the origin. Most of the items in the collection were sent from around the world as a gift to Horiyoshi, namely from other tattoo artists. Custom sheets of flash, signed to him, *With love and respect*, filled every inch of the walls.

There were so many items piled throughout the space that I couldn't even get close enough to view each relic in detail; I had to gaze from an angle and at a distance, squinting to read the tags the best I could. Next to Mayumi's desk stood a massive black and white photograph, tacked to the dirty horizontal blinds covering the windows. It hung unframed, unpreserved, and unpolished. It stood likely eight feet tall and six feet wide, blanketed in a light layer of dust, but its shine could not be dulled. The photograph was one I'd seen in my book many times; a larger-than-life-sized image of a younger Horiyoshi, turned on a slight angle. Half of his body waited deep in shadow while light had revealed the rest.

In the photograph, he wore only a *fundoshi*, a white cloth wrapped and tied around his loins. His frame statuesquely set on a backdrop of a black sheet tacked to a bookshelf within his own studio. He was a younger man than now, showing with stoicism his own bodysuit. My eyes focused on his left hand, fingers clenched tightly in a fist, but his face seemed so relaxed and confident. He looked past me with his gaze, and I could feel the calm power coming off of this photograph. Standing facing his naked body, I surveyed the image until it became only shapes. Half of the image appeared to actually be just plain black; I traced the side of his face with my eyes. Focusing on the deep crease between his nose and mouth, I touched my finger to this same spot on my own face.

Mayumi delicately rose from her station, and the movement awoke me into action again. She nodded at me as she exited the door, and I could hear her light footsteps treading to the private section of the second or third floor above me. Pulling my bag off my shoulders, I laid it on the ground next to her desk to move more freely throughout the packed space. I saw a sheet of flash containing four designs in bold, loose ink. It had been signed, *Love and respect, your friend, Teddy.* I recognized his youthful lines.

A smile drew my lips back, and I could feel the kitsune warm up my hip, telling me to shift into the shape of this moment. I sucked the heavy, stale air in through my nose and let it fill my lungs, opening my mouth only slightly to allow it to escape. I would not let the kitsune take me away fully; I am not a magical fox.

It's not what has happened to me to get me here. It's not what I deserve; it's simply what I got. I thought. You move your mouth and your arms and your legs and you tell yourself to walk through it, to scream through it, to run through it, to sleep through it. You give small pieces of yourself away to each person you meet; some take more than others. Some take so much without your permission. Some you give away freely without realizing that you cannot get it back. Then, you look at the clock, and you see the thousands upon thousands upon thousands of seconds that have passed, but they aren't gone. Rather, you're carrying them and trying to organize these moments in your mind, trying to cling on to so many and begging to forget others.

You are forced to go on with these thoughts to the very edge of the earth and put your toes over the cliff. Time tells you to walk off the solid surface and relieve yourself of this pressure to start fresh. You close your eyes and wish away the parts you want to forget. You try to sleep through the pain and block out the memories from coming to the surface. You want to stop the electricity in your brain that brings them to life and allows them to transform from an organism to a zygote. But you're not in control of this waking dream—time is. Time doesn't fade the past; it doesn't heal you, and it doesn't offer you an answer. It simply provides a catalog of thoughts that you cannot stop from being recalled, even if they happened so far in the past that they construct your reality. Your lens is smudged with these nanoseconds, and you're unable to select the filter you want.

Every person around you is viewing you through their time-riddled lens as well, so you touch their skin to see if the electricity will pass between your systems. Will this contact make your signal stronger, or will it try to suck the light and energy out of your vessel and use it to power its own? The answer is only at the edge, where you put your toes over the line of safety and ask for the relief you seek when you get there. You can only do this alone.

Hearing the door open, I turned my head to the bright entry. Half in shadow and half in the light, I saw a shape fill the frame. Older, softer, and gentler, my eyes searched the crease between his nose and mouth, recognizing this deep shape. No words would form in my throat.

"Hello," he said, bowing his head in my direction. His hair pulled back into a tight, grey ponytail, his shirt neatly tucked into his pants.

"Hi," I raised my hand to waist-height in a half-wave.

"Annalise," I offered, placing my hand over the center of my chest.

"Yes, Annalise," he repeated, his words well-formed, barely a hint of an accent.

"Can you see me?" I questioned. Not sure of where this thought came from. "Am I a ghost?" I raised my hands in front of myself, searching for the familiar lines of my wrists and fingers.

"You are very real," he smiled. He understood. "Come with me." He turned and headed back out the door.

I reached for my bag and followed behind his shadow up the stairs.

CHAPTER 43

"*G*hosts are real. I was painting one day in my Yokohama studio when I saw a figure walk in." His cadence was measured in his delivery, and his sentences were so perfectly formed. He looked just past my gaze as he spoke. "I turned to say hello, and it disappeared into black powder." He waved his hand into the air showing me how the ghost had dissipated. "I told this to a psychic, and he said that in the Meiji Era, there had once been an execution ground where I live, so there were lots of ghosts wandering around my neighborhood." He finished the conversation I'd started downstairs. "Ghosts, they are very real. But you, young woman, are not a ghost. Not yet." His glasses were slightly tinted, making it difficult for me to read his expression.

He presented very serious in nature, but open. He wore a long-sleeve black shirt, covering his collarbones and his wrists. He could have been a doctor. We were seated in the middle of his studio, kneeling on the mats laid on the floor.

The space was crowded full of books and drawings, and a few plants, organized but disheveled at the same time.

"Do you know about the *Itako*?" his eyes veiled behind his glasses.

I shook my head slightly, indicating that I had been unsure of what he spoke of.

He leaned forward, raising off his heels for a brief moment, adjusting his weight. Settling back into place, he pulled his glasses from his face, revealing his eyes. They were dark and watery in the corners. Not as bright as I'd expected.

"The Itako carry the spirits in Japan; they let you talk to them," he began. "The *Shinto*." His hand made a motion like a fish swimming upstream but aiming toward the sky. The dance of the ghost. "The Itako are always blind women; they get their powers from their blindness." He pressed his fingers into his eyelids, the back of his hands spotted with darkened pigment. "There are only a few left here, in Japan. They are very special Shaman. They train for three years, and they call out to the gods to channel the ghosts. They are deprived of sleep, starved of food, and made to have hundreds of buckets of ice-cold water poured over them. Still, they are strong. They reach the other world and can send your messages." He stared deeply into my gaze, seeing the weakness inside of me.

"They perform rituals to contact the dead," he said. "They scatter rice and salt, and they enter the body of the Itako."

Raising my hands, I crossed my arms over my chest to feel for the spirit in the room, ensuring they could not enter my body.

"After much coaxing, the spirit enters!" his voice jumped up with expression. "The Itako sings the *kudoki*, but this is the ghost singing through her. You can get your answers this way, the memories from life and where he has been since death, and you may ask him to leave, but that is up to him." His voice held steady, and his words came out slowly.

"How do you make sure the spirit is gone?" I asked, worried that by this conversation, we'd encouraged Dylan to stay in this room.

"A spell must be repeated three times by the Itako." Clearing his throat, he searched his mind for the words.

I remembered the ritual of the evil eye my Nonna used to perform—a spell to be broken, a tradition to be followed.

"*The old fox in the Shinoda woods, when he cries during the day, then he does not cry in the night.* This is the spell. Three times, and the ghost will leave." His hands folded over his knees.

"How can you know if you're healed?" I questioned. "What if you don't want the ghost to visit you anymore? What if you want to forget the ghost?" My voice fell quiet, afraid I would begin to cry.

He sat for a moment, considering my question. He reached forward and placed his hands over the mat between us, flat on the ground, filling up the space but careful not to touch me. This struck me, his boundaries, coming from a man that lays his hands onto strangers' naked flesh all day.

"A master knows his own mistakes and wants to erase the evidence. I heard of a swordsmith who was dying and ordered his apprentices to find and destroy all the swords he had made when he was younger. I wish I could do that with some of my earlier tattoos. Sometimes, we wish we could do this with people too."

Tears took over my calm and rolled from my eyes, but I wasn't ashamed to cry.

"It's easy to forget the people you don't need anymore. One day you wake up, and they aren't the first thought that comes to your mind. Until that day, you still need them." He drew his hands from the space between us and rubbed them methodically on his thighs as he spoke. "It is not possible to know if this is the best you will feel, the most repaired you can be, because tomorrow will arrive, and it could be better, and it could be worse."

He shrugged his shoulders up to his ears, indicating the unknown. "How do you know if you have woken up from a bad dream or if the dream is still happening? You don't. The only thing you can be sure of is the fact that you will not be the same when you wake up. We don't know how we survive storms. When the tsunami passes over everything, you recognize nothing will be the same, namely yourself. That is the only certain fact." He motioned his hand as if a wave appeared to be coming over his head.

I let a long breath out of my mouth and nose, letting my belly roll over the waist of my pants. Rubbing my fingers deep into my eyes, I pushed Dylan out of my mind, sending him away on the wave of the tsunami, pleading with him not to wash back to shore.

After a few moments, I heard him speak.

"I know why you have come here, Annalise." His voice sounded warm. I opened my eyes to examine him.

"Sir, respectfully, I doubt you have any idea why I am here." I pressed my hands together in a praying position in front of my chest.

I surrendered to him. Suddenly, my body felt struck by how surreal this moment became for me. *What was I doing here?* I thought.

"I . . . I am not sure what I am doing in this room," I stuttered. Aware of my body, of my gender, of my origin.

"What do you mean?" he probed, his voice raising with curiosity.

"How am I deserving of your time?" A scoff escaped from my throat unexpectedly. "Tattooers travel from every corner of the world; they save, they plan, and they crawl to your door to put a sticker on your window and speculate if you might be locked away up here, hovered over some lucky soul working on them. All the while, here I am, not even a tattooer, not even a tattooer's wife anymore, sitting in this room with you, Horiyoshi the Third, talking about fucking ghosts!" A laugh sharply flew from my mouth.

He chuckled, standing up. "You know you are deserving of any experience you are brave enough to create for yourself. It is that simple." He turned on his heel to walk to his shelf. "And Annalise, the one certainty that you must know is that no matter how far you have run away, you are always a tattooer's wife. A tattooer's widow." That word rolled in between us like a storm cloud. "I have been expecting your arrival, as a matter of fact" his tone sounded light, raising his eyebrows in anticipation of my reply.

"You, what?" I blurted out. "Not possible, you aren't an Itako! You are not an old blind ghost-talking woman!" My heart raced; I felt anxious that he could see into me. I pushed myself up onto my feet.

"No, you are correct. I cannot speak with ghosts." He tilted his chin to the ground.

"I spoke with Clive a few days ago, and he told me you were coming to see me. I've been waiting for you." His words were strong and purposeful; his hands cupped together at the waist.

"Clive?" I blurted out. "Clive?" I repeated the name again. What was he talking about?

"Yes, Clive. The Frenchy. He knew you'd be coming to see me next; he told me you'd be here to see the ginkgo trees."

Our eyes locked together, and it felt like a million pounds of sand had buried my body. I couldn't move my limbs. My ears were hot, the kitsune stirred on my leg, begging me to run. I froze in this space.

"He . . . he did?" I managed to whisper.

"Yes, he seemed very certain you were on your way. He informed me that you have a project that you need me to complete with you." His eyes danced over the cardboard tube tied to my backpack.

The Fudo Myo-o sprung into my mind, I could see not the drawing in my possession, but the version tattooed on Dylan's back; I pictured the eyes, haloed by burning fire peeking from the covers when I rolled over to face him in bed. I could see the shape of the Fudo's face distorted by the slope of Dylan's shoulder as his weight fell to his side. His shallow breathing in and out adding life to the Fudo. I reached my finger out and traced the line of the Fudo's sword down his body, causing him to stir, resting my hand on his hip. Pulling the white sheet over my head to block the sun that snuck in through the window, it was just Fudo and me together, our eyes locked.

How long until I forget this memory? I wondered. *I'd like to keep just this single moment in my mind.* I want to keep this one where my gaze can search the colors on his skin and focus on the pores and lines and patterns and details in silence—watching them move with the metered breathing. Watching silently, filtering the light through the sheet as Dylan and I shared the oxygen in the small tent I'd created between us, his skin so warm under my fingers.

"I . . . well . . . yes," I acknowledged that he had been right, confirming my purpose for being here.

"For some, getting tattooed is healing. To get a full-body tattoo takes years of suffering, and that requires maturing as a human, learning to experience and overcome pain. It is as if with each piercing of the needle, they become stronger and more complete. You have arrived to me fortified, strong, and ready." He spoke without effort but sounded like an orator with each sentence.

"A lot can change very quickly, you know," he said.

I walked to my bag and crouched to grab hold of the cardboard tube containing the drawings and stencils that had made this journey with me. I extended it to him, calmly. He pulled the end free and slid the fine papers out, the edges bouncing and curling as he smoothed his hands over them on the mats below.

"You and me, we cannot know what it means to die." His forehead was deep with lines as he raised his focus to meet my gaze. "We can only know what it means to want to add more minutes to the clock. This is what we are not capable of understanding in others. Can you imagine if you had to wear your soul on the outside for others to see? We would all feel so much shame. That is what tattooing is. It is wearing our souls on the outside so others can glimpse at who we are."

He paused, pulling the layers of papers apart until arriving upon the heavy drawing of the Fudo Myo-o.

"What we are searching for in others is to make up for the small parts of ourselves that we cannot find, and this is okay. You do not have to get this from others. You can get this from me, from this Fudo, from the three of us together. We will make you whole."

He grasped the edges of the paper and began to rise.

"I promise, I will not tell anyone what I see when I look into your soul, but I promise you, it will not be the darkest I've seen. You can leave behind whatever you need to here. That is the point."

With that, he turned and walked to his drawing table with the Fudo in hand, ready to prepare. To begin.

I felt the tsunami wave crest over my head; it caught my feet from under me and lifted me off the ground, but it could not carry me away.

"I am not a ghost," I replied.

I knew this much for sure.

Citations

Chapter 43 uses true quotes
from Horyoshi III as recorded by
Judit Kawaguhi's, *Words to Live
By* judittokyo.com

ACKNOWLEDGMENTS

A heartfelt thank you to the many folks that saw through this project with me, providing encouragement, technical know-how, and love along the way. To Andrew Buckley for the most patient relaying of the simple basics, and for fiercely editing a book in the despised literary fiction category. Keddy Pavlik, your detailed edits were just what I needed. My friends, Curtis McGrath, and the women who conjured The Black Egg—Whitney, Abbie, and Kerrie. Your support was noticed.

To my partner, Brian Joubert. The tattooer and motor-biker in my life that proofread for accuracy and details, read without judgment, and forced me to see this through. You cried more tears than me during the process of this book coming to life and weren't afraid to show compassion when it mattered. I never wanted to be a tattooer's wife, but how dull life would be otherwise. I would not have finished this project if you hadn't bullied me into it.

Lastly, and most important of all—Christa. This story started as an embryo created from your bold and everlasting sense of self. Your ability to live as the ultimate icon of female power makes you stand tallest in the darkest moments that life had to offer you. Your impact on others is immeasurable. You are a vector of creativity, an outspoken feminist, a delicate, gentle, thoughtful empath, and a woman that I aspire to evolve into. Healing happens with the gentle and loving line of a tattoo.

ABOUT THE AUTHOR

*B*ecky Parisotto is a tech executive by day, and a tattooer's wife and author of the new novel *The Tattoo Widow*, by night. Becky earned her Bachelor's of Creative & Critical Studies from the University of British Columbia, majoring in Fine Arts. She lives in Kelowna, BC, Canada with her husband, and their German Shepard, named Doug. She doesn't have any tattoos.

Connect with her online at thetattoowidow.com

CPSIA information can be obtained
at www.ICGtesting.com
Printed in the USA
LVHW010505201021
700870LV00005B/133

9 781039 112308